'Wow!'

Gina absorbed the solitude, the natural beauty, amazed by the clarity of the ocean—a glistening mix of emeralds and azures.

And at that moment it seemed as if a very sea-god appeared from behind the rocks, swimming towards the shore with an easy stroke before rising from the water. Gina gasped, wondering for a moment if the apparition was real or a figment of her imagination.

He certainly looked real. The sheer masculine perfection of him held her spellbound. As she watched, he ran the fingers of his free hand through jet-black hair, shedding water, sweeping the strands back from an arresting, impossibly handsome face. A face that could have been sculpted from the surrounding granite by the hand of a master craftsman. Yet he was undoubtedly flesh and blood…human and all male.

As he strode through the shallows to the beach Gina felt overheated, sure she would melt on the spot. Then he looked up, stilling as he noticed her for the first time. The breath trapped in her lungs as their gazes met. Her sea-god changed direction, walking purposefully towards her, the touch of his gaze firing her blood and tightening her stomach. With more haste than grace, Gina scrambled to her feet as he closed the last of the distance between them.

'Buongiorno, signorina.'

Margaret McDonagh says of herself: 'I began losing myself in the magical world of books from a very young age, and I always knew that I had to write, pursuing the dream for over twenty years, often with cussed stubbornness in the face of rejection letters! Despite having numerous romance novellas, short stories and serials published, the news that my first "proper book" had been accepted by Harlequin Mills & Boon for their Medical™ romance line brought indescribable joy! Having a passion for learning makes researching an involving pleasure, and I love developing new characters, getting to know them, setting them challenges to overcome. The hardest part is saying goodbye to them, because they become so real to me. And I always fall in love with my heroes! Writing and reading books, keeping in touch with friends, watching sport and meeting the demands of my four-legged companions keeps me well occupied. I hope you enjoy reading this book as much as I loved writing it.'

www.margaretmcdonagh.com
margaret.mcdonagh@yahoo.co.uk

Recent titles by the same author:

ITALIAN DOCTOR, DREAM PROPOSAL
THE REBEL SURGEON'S PROPOSAL
THE EMERGENCY DOCTOR CLAIMS HIS WIFE
DR DEVEREUX'S PROPOSAL*

Brides of Penhally Bay

AN ITALIAN AFFAIR

BY
MARGARET McDONAGH

First published in Great Britain 2008
This edition 2010
Harlequin Mills & Boon Limited,
Eton House, 18-24 Paradise Road, Richmond, Surrey TW9 1SR

© Margaret McDonagh 2008

ISBN: 978 0 263 21279 2

Harlequin Mills & Boon policy is to use papers that are natural,
renewable and recyclable products and made from wood grown in
sustainable forests. The logging and manufacturing process conform
to the legal environmental regulations of the country of origin.

Printed and bound in Great Britain
by CPI Antony Rowe, Chippenham, Wiltshire

AN ITALIAN AFFAIR

To my very special editor, Joanne…
Thank you so much for believing in me
and for giving me the chance
to fulfil my dreams.

To Fiona J…
Thank you for your support,
and for all your kindness and care.

PROLOGUE

A WOMAN'S scream—high-pitched and fearful—shattered the silence.

Sebastiano Adriani paused, his purposeful stride faltering, his gaze scanning the dark, narrow streets for the source of the sound. Concerned, he changed direction, heading further away from home to investigate. He could spare a few moments to ensure no one was in serious trouble.

In the early hours of the morning, Florence was quiet. Only a few street cleaners were in evidence, along with an occasional couple who lingered to embrace as they made their way home after a romantic night out. The July air was laden with sultry summer heat, so Seb had removed his tie, unfastened the top button of his shirt, and slung the jacket of his Armani suit over one arm. Despite the lateness of the hour, he had chosen to walk back to his expensive but impersonal apartment not far from the hospital. Both the exercise and the solitude appealed to him.

He had spent a pleasant enough evening escorting Lidia di Napoli, first to dinner at one of the city's finest restaurants, which boasted three Michelin rosettes, and then to an open-air classical concert. Not his normal taste in music, but Lidia, an attractive young actress, had pouted prettily and begged him to accompany her. Her pout had been less appealing later in the evening, when he had been called back to the hospital. A *pro bono* patient he had operated on that morning—a young man who had needed major and intricate facial reconstruction following a traffic accident—had taken a sudden and unexpected turn for the worse. Seb's presence had been needed urgently. To the relief of the medical team, the young man was now stable but under constant observation in intensive care.

Lidia had been vocally displeased at the abrupt end to the evening, and had still been complaining as he had paid a taxi to take her home...alone. If she hoped to see him again, she would need to learn that nothing and no one came before his work. Not that he would have stayed with her, regardless of the unsubtle inducements she had been offering since he had collected her from the theatre at the end of rehearsals for her new play. He never spent the night in any woman's bed—and never allowed a woman in his.

Thankfully, due to the latest political scandal to take Florence by storm, the paparazzi had been absent from the restaurant, tracking down more lucrative prey elsewhere. For once his evening, and his companion, had failed to attract media attention, and he had been able to eat dinner and attend the concert without being bothered. He was grateful. Unlike the women who tried to be seen on his arm, who sought to use his name to further their own, he had no desire to feature in the gossip columns.

Hearing raised voices, Seb increased his pace, cutting through a nearby *piazza* into a warren of narrow streets just as another scream alerted him to the panicked woman's location. Rounding a corner, he saw a man, dressed all in black, hit his victim in the face and begin dragging her struggling form towards a recessed doorway.

'Arresto!' Shouting at the man to stop, to leave her alone, Seb ran to the woman's aid. *'Lasci il sua solo!'*

Pushing the sobbing woman roughly aside, the assailant refocused his attention. Cautious, but unafraid, Seb faced the man. He knew how to look after himself. The outward veneer of polish and sophistication he now wore with ease, as one of Europe's most successful reconstructive plastic surgeons to the rich and famous, failed to mask his origins. The boy from the streets, who had survived on his charm and his wits, had never been entirely banished.

Jockeying for position, Seb placed himself between the attacker and the distressed woman, keeping her safe in the doorway behind him. Despite the paucity of light, Seb scanned the man's build and face, memorising every detail and distinguishing feature he could for later identification: the scar bisecting his chin, the letters tattooed in red across the knuckles of each hand, the row of gold studs outlining one ear. Never taking his attention from his opponent, Seb tossed the woman his mobile phone and instructed her to call the police. He had hoped the man would back down, but he appeared undaunted, moving swiftly, the sudden flash of a knifeblade a silvery menace in the shadows.

Adrenalin pumped through Seb's veins. Watchful and wary, he dodged to the side as the man lunged towards him, the knife extended. With his jacket wrapped around his right arm, Seb used the padding to deflect the next attack as the knife slashed sideways through the air. The fabric ripped. But not his skin. Yet. His heart was thudding under his ribs. Dimly, he was aware of the woman crying on the phone, giving their location, begging for help, but his sole focus was on the knife. Again the man came towards him. Again Seb attempted to deflect the blow. The material afforded scant protection, and he winced as the knife sliced across his wrist and bit into the heel of his right hand. He could feel the blood welling from the wounds, flowing hot and sticky down his palm and between his fingers.

In the distance came the wail of a siren, but the man refused to retreat, feinting one way and then the other in an attempt to get past Seb and reach the woman. She screamed again, pressing back into the corner of the doorway. Thinking only of protecting her, Seb stepped in front of the man once more. Keeping his voice calm, he told him to give up, reminding him the police were coming. The sirens were ever louder.

'Rinunziare. La polizia sta venendo.'

Swearing profusely, the man lunged forward a final time. As the knife came towards his face, Seb instinctively raised both arms to shield himself, the razor-sharp blade cutting through his left forearm near the inner elbow before slashing across his right wrist and palm. Seb kicked out, catching the man off balance. The attacker staggered back, cursing violently before he regained his footing. Then, with the police closing in, he ran from the scene, disappearing into the darkness.

Ignoring his own problems, Seb turned to check that the woman was all right. *'Signora, come sta?'*

'Bene. Grazie, Signor, mille grazie.' The woman sobbed her thanks. *'Dio! Siete sanguinando!'*

Seb already knew he was bleeding. Assured that the woman was physically unharmed, he dropped to his knees, anxious to attend to his wounds, to stem the blood and keep his hands—the tools of his trade—elevated to reduce any swelling. His injuries produced a worrying mix of pain and numbness. And he couldn't perform the actions he intended. His left arm felt heavy and sluggish, refusing to transmit his commands to his hand. His right wrist was slack, and the thumb and index finger of his right hand wouldn't move, couldn't grasp the tissues the woman handed him.

He had not been scared before.

Now he was.

CHAPTER ONE

'I AM sure we found the right place, Gina. The special place I shared with my Matteo.'

Gina McNaught heard the emotion in her grandmother's familiar accented voice. A mixture of wistfulness, anxiety and longing brought a gleam to faded hazel eyes, while a fierce determination radiated from the elderly lady's increasingly frail frame. Once long ebony hair was now short and grey—more evidence of the relentless march of time. Smiling against the melancholy realisation that there might not be many more years, Gina took one work-roughened hand in hers and gave a gentle squeeze. She knew what this journey meant to her grandmother...knew how important it was that they located the exact spot depicted in the faded black and white photograph now resting on the table in front of them.

The photograph, and the story accompanying it, had intrigued and enchanted Gina since she had been a young child. She never tired of hearing how fate had brought her Italian grandmother and her Scottish grandfather together, how Maria Tesotto and Matthew McNaught had met on a deserted beach...and had fallen in love.

'There was no villa there in those days,' her grandmother continued, lost in her memories. 'But it is still secluded, unspoilt...and the name gives it away, no? Back then, people referred to the rock in the sea as Lancia del Nettuno—Neptune's Spear. You can just see it in the picture. And now we find Villa alla Roccia del Nettuno. The Villa at Neptune's rock. Gina, it *has* to be right.'

'I'll find out, Nonna. I promise.'

'You do so much for me, *ragazza mia*. Maybe too much, no?' she asked with a sad smile.

'Of course not,' Gina reassured her. 'You mean the world to me.'

One increasingly arthritic hand cupped her cheek. 'And you to me. But I worry that you have given up so much of your own life for me...and for your grandfather. Since we left that damp old council house in Glasgow and came to live with you in your lovely cottage in Strathlochan you have spent all your time caring for us and making our lives comfortable when you are not working at the hospital.'

'Nonna—'

'I know.' Her grandmother forestalled the interruption. 'You see your friends. You love your job. But there is more to life, Gina. We never wanted you to end your relationship with Malcolm because of us.'

Gina ducked her head to hide her gaze. No way would she ever tell her grandmother the vicious, hurtful things Malcolm had said. 'It wasn't like that, Nonna. Things had run their course.' They had certainly been over when she had discovered that Malcolm's understanding of family and her own were so widely divergent.

'But it's four years, and you've not dated at all! I want you to be happy—as happy as I was for all those years with my Matteo. I want you to find that special man who is right for you. You should be meeting men, having fun, thinking of your own needs.'

Perhaps it was being back on Elba, where her own happiness had begun, that had put these ideas into her grandmother's head. 'I'm fine, Nonna.'

It was a long time since she had allowed herself to have

needs, or to indulge in dreams of her own. Real life hadn't worked out that way. Not for her. And maybe, having grown up with the fairytale, she couldn't bring herself to settle for anything less. She had made her choices and she had no regrets…even if she could scarcely remember how it felt to be a desirable woman.

'Now you give up your holiday time and organise this trip, obliging the whim of an old woman.'

The words pulled Gina from her reverie. 'That's nonsense and you know it,' she rebuked softly. 'Besides, I have always longed to see Elba. What better place could we come together?' She smiled, but the reason for their visit here took the gloss off her pleasure, as did the sadness that dulled the light in her grandmother's eyes.

'That is true. And you would have found a way to bring me here no matter what, keeping the promise you made to me and your grandfather. This means so much to me.'

'I know, Nonna.' Gina hid her worry about the toll this trip might take on a woman troubled by her aging, arthritic body, not to mention the emotions involved by returning to the place she held so dear while bearing the loss of the man who had been her world for fifty years. 'Will you be all right resting here on your own if I go back and see if someone has returned to the villa?'

Her grandmother patted her hand. 'Do not fret. I am fatigued after our long hours of travel yesterday, that is all.'

The journey, entailing a flight from Scotland to Pisa, and then a train ride to Piombino, the port on the Italian mainland from where they had caught the ferry to Portoferraio, Elba's capital town, had been exhausting. And it had not ended until they had travelled to the unspoilt western end of the mountainous island, where Gina had booked a room at an inexpensive bed and breakfast run from a private house. The twin-bedded room was small, basic, but comfortable…all she could afford on a tight budget.

It was also close to Capo Sant'Andrea, a name her grandmother remembered, believing it to be near their ultimate destination. Gina wasn't surprised her grandmother, now seventy years old, was feeling the strain—especially as she had insisted they begin their search for the right location along the stretch of the north-west coast first thing that morning. Thanks to the taxi driver's local knowledge, they had struck lucky and found the hidden cove containing Neptune's Spear. Gina could only hope that her grandmother would not be disappointed with the rest of her quest.

'I'll go and make enquiries.' Rising to her feet, Gina collected her bag. 'My mobile phone number is on the pad, and Signora Mancini has it, too. She'll be here if you need anything.' She was grateful to their kindly landlady, who had volunteered to maintain a discreet watch while Gina was out. Her grandmother nodded, masking a couple of coughs, and Gina frowned, unable to dismiss a twinge of unease. Bending, she kissed a soft, wrinkled cheek, sending up a silent wish that her outing would be successful. 'I'll do my best for you, Nonna.'

'You always do. Bless you, *ragazza mia*.'

Moisture shimmered in wise hazel eyes and Gina forced a smile, blinking back the answering tears that pricked her own darker eyes. 'I'll see you soon.'

Keen to cut costs where possible, Gina declined the taxi that had been necessary that morning with her grandmother's decreased mobility. Instead, she hired a bicycle and rode back along the narrow, winding roads of the cape towards the villa their search had identified earlier in the day.

All her twenty-eight years money had been tight, but what the McNaughts had lacked in material things had been more than compensated for with an abundance of love, care and support. She had revelled in being able to return that love and care by having her grandparents live with her for the last four years, seeing them benefit from Strathlochan's cleaner air, cosier conditions and sense of community. Any thought that she had put a part of her life on hold to do it she pushed to the back of her mind. She had made her choices and had never had a moment of regret. Now, though, her grandfather was gone, and the pain of his loss stabbed through her. Her grandparents had never been able to return to Italy together, but she had vowed to help her grandmother see this through.

With only her nursing salary, it was a struggle to pay all the bills, to cover her mortgage and to meet her grandmother's needs. The elderly lady's pension was a pittance and, despite a lifetime of hard work, her grandfather had been able to leave little behind in support. She had a small amount left in an emergency fund, but Gina prayed she wouldn't need to use it—and that Nonna Maria wouldn't find out that she had cashed in her savings to pay for this Elban pilgrimage.

Coming to a halt at the entrance to the villa, Gina paused a moment. Taking in a breath of clean air, she marvelled at the landscape, at the way chestnut woods swept down the hillsides to the coast. All was quiet. She stared at the sign on the gate across the drive that led to a home hidden from view amongst the trees. Villa alla Roccia del Nettuno. The Villa at Neptune's Rock. For her grandmother's sake, Gina hoped this was the right place—and that the owner would be understanding of the unusual request she had come here to make.

Closing the gate behind her, Gina pushed the bike up the rough driveway. She was glad she had worn trainers with her denim shorts and cut-off T-shirt, but when the villa finally came into view she worried that she was too casually dressed to make the right impression. Whoever lived here clearly didn't have money worries.

'Wow!'

She stared in admiration. Long and low, the palatial villa had a classic Elban red-tiled roof, while the walls were painted a pale creamy yellow. The garden was lush, the hilly terrain and native woodland lending perfect seclusion and privacy to the setting. The sound of birds and the faintest rustling of a breeze in the trees were the only noises to impinge on the silent stillness of the afternoon. Gina immediately felt at peace here, experiencing a strange sense of belonging. She wasn't given to fancy, but she wondered if she was close to the place that was so special to her grandparents, if she somehow sensed their spirits here, reaching across the ages.

Shaking her head at such a notion, she propped her bike against the wall, took her bag from the basket and hooked the strap over her shoulder. She walked to the front door, disappointed when no one answered her ring of the bell.

Undecided, she hesitated. They had come a long way, and this mission was important to her grandmother. She couldn't give up now. Perhaps she should wait for someone to return. She could leave a note, asking for the owner to phone, but she would rather explain her purpose for coming here in person. Feeling guilty for trespassing, she walked around the side of the villa. It was huge, a U-shape around a rear terrace, and it looked as if her whole cottage would fit into a couple of rooms here. The spacious terrace had a large table, comfortable chairs and recliners, plus an outdoor cooking facility. Near the far end was an artist's easel and equipment, but she didn't venture across the terrace to inspect the canvas. It was the view over the rocky cliffs and the sea that held her attention and took her breath away. She had never seen anything so stunning—and that was saying something, given the spectacular scenery around Strathlochan.

Drawn despite her caution, she followed a path through the shrubs which led to steep stone steps that marked the way down to a sheltered beach far below. This must be where Maria and Matthew had walked together fifty years ago, before the villa had been built. She had to go down there. Had to see for herself the precious cove, the rock formation shaped like Neptune's spear, the spot where her grandparents' love had been born.

It was a daunting trip down the uneven cliff steps, and Gina knew that if this did turn out to be the right place there was no way her grandmother would be able to manage the journey down. Once on the small crescent of beach, protected by the curving cliff walls, she had her first proper glimpse of the rock feature that rose from the water a distance offshore. Irregular, and surrounded by other rock forms, it did, indeed, look like a massive trident…Neptune's three-pronged spear…just as her grandparents had described so vividly and with so much fondness.

Gina absorbed the solitude, the natural beauty, amazed by the clarity of the water, a glistening mix of emeralds and azures. Sitting down, she wrapped her arms around her knees. The September sunshine was hot on her skin, and she tipped her head back, closing her eyes, imagining the moment her grandparents had met, the secret romantic rendezvous that had followed, their determination to marry despite Maria's parents' dissent. Maria and Matthew had made it work, had survived the hardships to enjoy a lifetime of devotion. All thanks to that one chance meeting on this tiny Elban beach.

Elba. The name had a magic to it. A magic sparked to life in her childhood as her grandmother regaled her with stories of this special place. Gina would never forget the moment yesterday when she had seen Elba for the first time. The mountainous outline of the island, jutting from the blueness of the sea, had shimmered into her vision and grown into reality. All her life she had been captivated by the romance, the fairytale, the joy and love that coloured her grandparents' memories of this place. She had been determined to come—one day. Now she was here. But in these circumstances?

Frowning, she turned her thoughts to the reason for bringing her grandmother back to Elba. She was concerned that the emotion would be too much, but her grandmother was determined, and Gina would never break the promises

she had made. Lulled by the peacefulness of the surround-
ings, she relaxed, some of the tension and responsibility
she had shouldered for so long draining from her.

The soft swell of the sea under the sun cast shifting light
over the rock formation, highlighting a myriad of colours
and textures. At that moment, as she stared towards the
mythical symbol, it seemed as if the very sea-god himself
appeared from behind the rocks, swimming towards the
shore with an easy stroke before rising from the water. Gina
gasped, startled from her reverie, wondering for a moment
if the apparition was real or a figment of her imagination.

He certainly looked real as he removed his mask and
snorkel and waded towards the beach at a slight angle
away from her. The sheer masculine perfection of him held
her spellbound. As she watched, he ran the fingers of his
free hand through jet-black hair, shedding water, sweeping
the strands back from an arresting, impossibly handsome
face. A face that could have been sculpted from the surrounding granite by the hand of a master craftsman. Yet he
was undoubtedly flesh and blood…human and all male.
Gina couldn't drag her gaze away from his athletic
physique, appreciating the broad shoulders, the bronzed
skin on which a sheen of water glistened, the supple
muscles, and a chest dusted with dark hair trailing in a
narrow line over a flat abdomen to his navel. Black swim-
shorts sat low on his hips, the wet fabric clinging to strong,
leanly muscled thighs.

As he strode through the shallows to the beach, Gina felt
overheated, sure she would melt on the spot. Then he
looked up, stilling as he noticed her for the first time. The
breath trapped in her lungs as their gazes met. Her sea-god
changed direction, walking purposefully towards her, the
touch of his gaze firing her blood and tightening her
stomach. With more haste than grace, Gina scrambled to
her feet as he closed the last of the distance between them.

   '*Buongiorno, signorina.*'

His accented voice was throaty and attractive, the warm huskiness of it sending prickles of awareness down her spine. Gathering her scattered wits, she answered in Italian.

'*Buongiorno.*'

It was hard to believe possible, but close up he was even more gorgeous than her first impression had suggested. Around six feet tall, she guessed he was in his early thirties. A day's growth of beard shadowed a strong, masculine jaw, while his mouth was sultry, beautifully shaped, his lips deliciously kissable. He had eyes the colour of liquid caramel, deeper than hazel, but not as dark a brown as her own, and they were framed by impossibly long sable lashes and gentle laughter lines.

Unable to resist the temptation, her gaze slid down to inspect his bare torso...strong shoulders, perfect chest, and a taut abdomen and belly. The way water droplets drizzled in slow motion down his dusky skin mesmerised her. She was so close to him that when she breathed in she inhaled the teasing scent of the sea, mingled with his woodsy male aroma. She had to fight the overwhelming urge to reach out and touch him.

Startled by her impulsive desire, Gina took a step back, her gaze lifting to his face, finding that he appraised her with equal thoroughness. Her breathing was uneven, her pulse raced, and her flesh tingled as if he had physically touched her. Alarmed, she retreated another pace. How long was it since she had appreciated an attractive man? How long since anyone had made *her* feel attractive and womanly?

'This is a private beach, *signorina*.'

The softness of his voice failed to mask the challenge and thread of accusation. 'I'm sorry,' she murmured, keeping to Italian, caught off guard by his sudden appearance as well as by her spontaneous reaction to him.

'How did you find it? What are you doing here?' he queried, folding his arms across his chest.

'Um...' Gina hesitated, distracted by the way his muscles

flexed as he moved. She forced herself to remember why she was here, determined to get back on track. 'Does the beach belong to the people who own the villa?'

Suspicion appeared in watchful eyes. 'Why does this interest you?'

'I need to talk to the owner.'

The man observed her for a moment, his expression unreadable. 'The villa is not for sale.'

'No. No, that's not it. I…'

'The property is owned by a family from Florence,' he informed her as her words trailed off. 'They are not expected to return to the island for some time.'

'So you take care of the place for them?' she mused to herself, wondering how much to confide in him, deflated as the prospect of a successful outcome began to crumble and the fulfilment of her grandmother's hopes began to fade.

A speculative glint appeared in his eyes. 'Tell me why you want to talk to them.'

'It's private.'

'Maybe I can help you.'

She regarded him warily. His presence made her feel breathless and shaky. 'If you'll tell me how I can contact the owners, *that* would help.'

'Come on up to the villa. We will talk. You will tell me why you want to find them, and I will consider giving you the information you need,' he suggested, tempting her with a lifeline to keep her promise to her grandparents alive.

Gina bit her lip, thinking of her grandmother and the reason they had come all this way. She couldn't let her down. And, with only a few days available to them before their return to Scotland, time was short. As caretaker, and with access to the owners of the beach, there was a chance this man could help her achieve her aim and grant her grandmother's appeal. Instinct warned her that spending more time in his company wasn't sensible, but it seemed she needed to work with him.

Her decision made, she nodded. 'All right. But I can't be too long. Someone is waiting for me.'

A man?

Seb frowned, wondering why the possibility bothered him so much. It was true that this unknown woman immediately intrigued him, with her mix of mystery and understated sexiness. Emerging from his swim to find the stranger on the beach had been a surprise—one he planned to explore to the fullest. Her presence made him suspicious. She had yet to explain how she had found the secluded villa, what she had been doing on the private beach, or what she wanted with his family. That she assumed him to be the caretaker could be genuine. He scanned her soul-deep brown eyes, searching for the truth. Or it could be the ruse of a clever journalist to lull him into a false sense of security and get a story on him. He had been tricked before. This time he would not let down his guard...or let this woman out of his sight...until he knew more about her and her motives.

Not that having her in his sight was a hardship. Far from it. He indulged in another leisurely perusal. In her mid to late twenties, and above average height, she had sultry dark eyes and flawless skin. Her hair was constrained in a loose braid that fell almost to her waist, its colour a rich deep brown, glinting with auburn highlights in the sun. He wanted to free it from its restraint and see the thick, lustrous waves in all their glory. Her facial features were strong yet feminine: a well-defined jawline with a hint of stubbornness in the set of her chin, high cheekbones, small, straight nose, and the kind of mouth that could tempt a man to wickedness...pouting, rosy-red lips demanding to be kissed with thorough abandon.

He was bored with the artificiality and falseness of the women he usually came into contact with, and this woman's natural freshness and apparent lack of affectation appealed to him. So did her shapely figure. Here was a woman with generous curves. Curves that were all her own, not fashioned on an operating table. She was voluptuous, earthy, comfortable in her skin. No wedding or engagement rings, he noticed, disconcerted by the rush of male satisfaction and possessiveness that observation brought. Indeed, she wore no jewellery or adornments at all...save for a simple narrow-banded silver watch around her right wrist.

Totally feminine, she stirred his interest as no other woman had ever done. But was she genuine? Could he trust her? Time would tell. For now, he wasn't anywhere near ready to let her go. Until he knew for sure who she was and what she wanted he would follow the maxim of keeping his friends close and any possible enemies closer.

Seb would have enjoyed a much longer inspection of her delectable body, but she readjusted the position of her canvas shoulder bag, then turned and headed towards the age-old steps cut into the cliff that led back up to the villa. Seb followed, appreciating the back view nearly as much as the front. Her faded denim shorts were cut well enough for him to enjoy the delicious swell of her rear, and short enough to allow a generous view of smooth, pleasingly rounded thighs. She moved a few steps up ahead of him, and he could admire gently muscled calves and trim ankles. Closing the distance between them, lured by the sway of her hips and the gentle bob of the plait hanging down her back, he resisted the temptation to brush his fingertips across the tantalising band of golden skin exposed between the low-slung shorts and the hem of her short-sleeved top. He was further intrigued by the small tattoo of a leaping dolphin at the base of her spine.

They were not quite halfway up the rough climb when a loose patch of ground came away under the woman's foot. Seb reacted instinctively to her startled cry, thankful he was close enough to catch her as she slipped precariously towards the edge. His heart was thudding as he dragged her back with him, holding her close as they leaned on the cliff wall for a moment, catching their breath.

'Thank you,' she gasped, resting against him, one fist closed around the strap of her bag, her other hand clinging to the rock face.

'Are you all right?'

She nodded. 'I'm fine.'

Still neither of them moved. Enjoying the feel of her in his arms, Seb was in no hurry to let go. One forearm rested under the lush fullness of her breasts, their plumpness, firm but soft, pressing against him. He could feel that the rapid thud of her heart matched his own. And as he breathed in he inhaled the scent of vanilla and sweet, sun-warmed woman. Sexy and arousing. Her body was athletic, strong, yet softly feminine. His free hand had settled at her bare navel, his fingertips brushing the silkiness of her skin.

Loosing her hold on the rock, she turned in his arms, on a level with him due to the incline of the steps. Their gazes locked. Time stopped. Seb's gaze dropped to her mouth. The urge to kiss her was almost irresistible. Almost. But suspicions still nagged at him. He didn't yet know if he could trust this woman. It took a huge effort of will to control his compulsive rush of desire, but he reluctantly released her and put a few inches of distance between them.

'We should move on,' he told her, cursing the uneven-ness of his voice.

Sooty lashes lowered to hide the expression in dark brown eyes. 'Yes.'

'Be careful how you go.'

As she turned from her rescuer and began making her way up the remainder of the steps to the top of the cliff, Gina intended to heed the warning. And not just in terms of watching her footing. Her reaction to the man himself was troubling. Her heart hammered and every particle of her thrummed—more from the feel of his body pressed against hers than from her stumble on the uneven ground. His strength, his heat, the male scent of him, had combined to make her light-headed. The warmth of his palm and the touch of his fingers on her bare skin had set her aflame. For one wild moment, when she had looked into those inscrutable eyes, she had thought he was going to kiss her. Even more disturbing was her yearning for him to do so. How long had it been since she'd been kissed?

Grateful to reach the safety of the path, she headed back towards the villa, conscious of his presence behind her. She felt shaken by her intense and instant attraction to the stranger who had emerged so unexpectedly from the sea. A tremor rippled through her as he rested a hand at the small of her back and guided her towards the expansive rear terrace with its incredible views.

'Make yourself comfortable, *signorina*.' His voice was polite but guarded as he gestured towards the chairs. 'Excuse me while I change. When I return, we will talk.'

'And you'll help me get in touch with the villa's owner?' she interjected, reminding him of her purpose, determined not to be defeated.

A smile played at his mouth, but suspicion still lurked in his eyes. 'We will see.'

The comment made Gina realise that she might have to confide more than she had intended if she hoped to gain his co-operation.

She watched him stride to the villa and disappear through a doorway. A sigh escaped her. She felt edgy, unsettled, and whilst she knew in part it was because of the importance of her mission here, she also knew that most of her jitters were due to the immediate desire she had experienced the moment she had met her enigmatic host. There was no denying her response to him, nor the masculine interest in his eyes as he had looked at her. She was shocked, because those few moments of mutual interest had cracked open a shell she had thought firmly con-structed, awakening things she had tamped down and rejected for herself when she had made the decision to put her grandparents' needs before her own. Maybe she was allowing the setting and the fairytale of their romance here to go to her head. That was all it was, she consoled herself. When she saw the man again things would be fine, the mo-mentary aberration would have passed.

Unable to keep still, she set her bag on the table, then walked to the balustrade wall, leaning on it to admire the sweep of coast laid out before her. Curiosity bettered her, and she moved along to the artist's easel she had noticed earlier, stepping closer to inspect the canvas. The work was unfinished but impressive, the style unusual. She was no expert, but the clever use of abstract blocks making up the seascape appealed to her. She wondered if her sea-god was the artist, or if someone else lived here with him. A woman?

A noise alerted her that she was no longer alone. Embarrassed at being caught snooping, she spun round. Several things hit her at the same time. Any hope that her reaction to him had been a passing fancy was instantly dis-counted. Dressed in leg-hugging jeans and a black T-shirt, the man was darkly attractive and dangerously exciting, his impact no less disconcerting now he was fully dressed. He had taken time for a quick shave, but he was just as ruggedly appealing as before, with an untamed air that did strange things to her hormones. Hormones that were meant to be in retirement, or at least a long hibernation.

Carrying two glasses containing some kind of fruit drink, he was frowning as he approached. Instead of setting them both down together, he put the glass in his left hand on the table before transferring the second from his right hand to his left. Puzzled by his awkwardness, she noted the way he attempted to flex his right wrist, index finger and thumb, as if experiencing problems with movement, maybe numbness or pain. It was as she neared him that she noted for the first time the fresh scars that marred his skin...three across the palm, heel and wrist of his right hand, one on his left forearm near his inner elbow.

Her caring nature rose to the fore, and she wanted to help, to comfort, but one look at the challenge and flare of angry pride in his eyes kept her questions and her concern unspoken. Experience as a trauma nurse helped her mask her emotions and interested speculation. Ignoring what she suspected he would see as his weakness, she made no comment and sat down.

'Thank you for the drink, *signor*.' She smiled, taking a sip of the tangy mixed berry juice from the glass nearest her. 'It's very refreshing. The weather is still so warm here.'

He inclined his head, a momentary flash of puzzlement crossing his expression before he drew out the chair next to her and sat far too close, heightening her intense awareness of him. 'You are welcome. And now that you are officially my guest, and I am to try to help you, we should introduce ourselves.'

'Yes, of course.' Setting down her glass, suppressing a shiver of anticipation at the thought of touching him again, she held out her hand. 'My name is Gina. Gina McNaught.'

'I am pleased to meet you, Gina.'

The way he said her name caused a fresh tingle of desire to chase along her spine. Then his hand sought hers, and every nerve-ending was focused on his touch, on the way his strong but graceful fingers curled around her own, the pad of his thumb brushing across the back of her hand like a caress. As her palm was all but swallowed up in his, she felt the jagged lines of the scars he had suffered, wondering again what had happened to him.

'And your name is...?' She faced him, hoping her voice had been steady and he wouldn't realise the effect he had on her.

For a moment he returned her gaze in silence, the ex-pression in his eyes unreadable save for a glimmer of that masculine pride and challenge. 'I am Sebastiano Adriani.'

CHAPTER TWO

NOT a flicker of recognition showed in Gina's eyes at the mention of his name, Seb noted. Either she genuinely had no idea who he was, or she was an exceptionally good actress. He was not prepared to take any chances. Why had she come here? *Was* she a journalist out for an exclusive story? Or a woman on the make, wanting to use his name, his money, to further her own ends?

When he had gone inside to change his clothes, he had glanced out the front door, expecting to find the car Gina had arrived in. Hoping for clues, maybe a Florentine number plate that could suggest she had followed him here, he had been surprised to discover instead a rented tourist bike propped against the wall. It added to the woman's mystery. And it crossed his mind that the bike could be a crafty prop. Life had taught him to be cynical and untrusting.

Gina refused to fit into a convenient box in his head. Nothing about her and her sudden appearance on the beach made sense. Nor could he explain her reaction to his awkwardness with the drinks. He knew she had noticed the scars that reminded him at every moment of how his life had changed. Most people in the last weeks had shied away from touching him—even talking to him. They either refused to mention what had happened, as if that would make it go away, or they patronised him, treating him like an invalid. Gina was different. She had not fussed, had not been embarrassed, and had not hesitated in instigating the handshake.

Needing time to think how to handle this situation, how to draw out the information he needed to know from her while giving nothing of himself away, he followed her lead and settled back to enjoy the view. But as he reached out to pick up his drink his hand locked again. It happened sometimes, often when he was least prepared for it. He hated it. Hated even more for his clumsiness to be witnessed.

As he cursed under his breath, Gina calmly rescued the glass and set it back on the table. Seb froze as she boldly took his right hand in both of hers. Since the incident that July night in Florence, people had pitied him, or smothered him, unable to face the reality. He braced himself, but Gina surprised him by tackling the issue head on.

'How long has it been, Sebastiano?' she asked, stripping away his defences with the exquisite gentleness of her touch, the understanding, concern and complete lack of pity in her eyes.

'Seb,' he corrected, thrown off balance by this woman. His voice sounded rough, and he tried to shut his mind to the vivid memories of that night. 'Seven weeks.'

Gina refused to back down. 'What happened?'

Unable to comprehend why he was telling her anything at all, he found himself playing down his role in the incident, passing off his injuries as an accident while going to the aid of the woman being attacked. From her expression, Gina knew there was more to it, but she didn't press him. Dark thoughts assailed him as he recalled how he had staved off blows to his face and body, but at the expense of the knife slicing through his hand and arm. The resulting loss of sensory and motor function, while not impacting significantly on his normal daily existence, was sufficient to prevent him from carrying out the intricate surgery that was his life.

In his heart he had known from the moment he had knelt on that dark street as the police had arrived and the frightened woman had fussed over him that he was finished as a surgeon. All he had been able to focus on was his hands, and the fear that no matter how quickly he got to hospital the damage was done. He had been right. He would never operate again.

Throughout his time in plaster he had gone along with family and colleagues who had assured him everything would be all right. Inside he had known it would not. His moment of selflessness had robbed him of the thing that mattered to him most. His career was over. Many other things were over, too, he allowed with cynicism. How many so-called friends had faded away these last weeks? How many celebrity clients had blanked him now he was no longer of use to them? How many women, like vain, fickle Lidia di Napoli, once eager for the kudos of being associated socially with him, had vanished like rats deserting a sinking ship? He was no longer the darling of Florentine society. Only the media, eager to capture the gory details of his descent from the pinnacle of his profession, still chased him.

As soon as he had been able to cope alone, he had left his aunt and uncle's house and come to the family villa on Elba, to escape the press and decide what the hell he was going to do with the rest of his life. Here on the island he could be himself. No one bothered him. The locals knew and respected the family, guarding their privacy. And, thankfully, the press had never found this place. Or had they? Did that explain the presence of his unexpected visitor?

'It must have been a terrible experience, Seb.'

Gina's comment interrupted his runaway thoughts, and his suspicions about her intensified. 'You could say that.'

Unfazed by his sarcasm, she studied his scars. 'Nerve and tendon damage?'

'Yes.'

He started as one finger brushed across the scar on the inside of his left forearm near the indentation of the elbow. The feather-light touch sent darts of awareness shooting through him.

'Does this cause you problems, too? Was the ulnar nerve cut here?'

'Why?' Who *was* this woman? Did she know more about him than she was pretending? 'What do you know about it?'

Dusky lashes lifted and dark brown eyes looked into his own, a self-deprecating smile curving her tempting mouth. 'Sorry. I'm being nosy. I didn't mean to intrude. It's an occupational hazard. I'm a senior staff nurse, and until a few days ago I worked in a busy accident and emergency department.'

That explained her knowledgeable questions, Seb allowed, but left more of his own unanswered. She was a nurse who had recently worked in trauma. Had she known where he was and thought to…what? Care for him? Heaven forbid. Or was she hoping to find a new job working on his team? She would be out of luck. He no longer *had* a team. Seb opened his mouth to tell her it was a waste of time, looking to him to aid her career, but it seemed her inquisitiveness had not yet ended.

'Are you having physio? Keeping up the mobility is important, as you'll find you can regain more sensation and movement for many months yet.' She awarded him another smile, her fingers sure but gentle as they explored his hand. 'I'm sure your surgeon has already told you that. Injuries like this weren't unusual in the department I worked in, and I know how frustrating it can be in the early stages of recovery. Don't lose heart on there not being more improvement to come. Are you the artist?'

'Sorry?' Her chatter and her sudden change of subject amused and vexed him at one and the same time.

Gina gestured across the terrace to his unfinished canvas, and he remembered she had been looking at it when he had come out of the villa. 'Is the painting yours?'

'Yes. I wanted to see if I could still handle the brushes. I can't grip properly, so I've had to change my style, but—'

Seb broke off, annoyed with himself for revealing more to this woman. How did she *do* that? How could she slip inside his protective shell and make him say things, do things, he never would with anyone else? Realising she was still holding his hand, that he was allowing her to do so, he frowned and removed it, even more cross with himself for missing her touch.

Undaunted by his gruffness, she took another sip of her drink. 'The painting is different, but in a good way. Interesting. Atmospheric.'

'You like it?' Surprise drew the question from him.

'It's amazing. Cleverly done with those abstract blocks or zones. You've captured the sharpness of the natural light and the vivid colours of the island to perfection. Do you sell a lot to tourists?'

'No.'

'You should. I'm sure your work would be very popular.'

Watching her, Seb wondered if she was as uncomplicated and as innocent as she seemed. Did she really believe him to be the villa's caretaker—a man who sold a few paintings to supplement his income? It could be a front, a cover for why she was here, but gut reaction nagged at him that she was telling the truth. He would be checking out her story once he learned more about her, but she was so open, so completely without guile, that it would surprise him were she not genuine. Having been caught out before, however, he couldn't take any chances now.

Determined to wrest back control of this situation, he set about asking some questions of his own.

'You said you worked in trauma. Are you here looking for a new job?' He watched her closely as she absorbed his words.

'No, not at all.' She tossed her braid over her shoulder. 'I start in my new role as soon as I get home.'

Her smile increased in wattage and did curious things

to his insides. He wondered whether he would wake up any moment and discover this strange interlude had been some surreal dream—that Gina was a figment of his imagination. So much for taking charge of things. Sitting forward, he rested his forearms on his knees.

'And where is home, Gina?'

'Strathlochan.' His confusion must have been obvious because she laughed. 'It's in Scotland.'

That threw him. As did the place name. Why did Strathlochan sound familiar? He had never been to Scotland. But his cousin Riccardo had. He made a mental note to check the connection with him later. Several other facts hit him at the same time. Gina's surname should have registered with him before, yet her colouring betrayed a Latin ancestry, and she spoke Italian like a native. He needed to probe more deeply into this intriguing woman's background, and get to the bottom of just what she had been doing on the villa's private beach.

'You do not live on Elba?' Seb questioned, and Gina sensed his surprise.

'No. I've always lived in Scotland,' she confirmed, keeping to Italian. 'I'm only here for a short holiday.'

'Your Italian is perfect,' Seb countered, in proficient if accented English.

'As is your English.' She was startled by his fluency. Knowing she would have to divulge more about herself if she was to secure his help, she continued. 'I have Italian ancestry, but I have never been here before.'

His watchful gaze held her captive. 'You are enjoying Elba? The island is beautiful, no?'

'Very beautiful.'

She couldn't look away from him to appreciate the coastal view. His nearness and his attention were potent, firing her blood and increasing the awareness she had felt from the first moment she had seen him. She remained curious about his injuries, convinced there was more to the incident than he had told her. He'd put himself in danger to go to someone's aid, and no matter how much he tried to play down his involvement, that said a great deal about him in her view. But the pain, anger and confusion evident in his eyes attested to the fact that he had yet to come to terms with the effect his loss of motor and sensory function had had on his life.

It must be hard for him as an artist, worrying whether he would be able to use his hands again. She would like to reassure him, but he put up barriers, retreated behind his pride. He was not a man to share the troubled feelings she sensed boiled inside him. Besides, it was none of her business. After today she would probably never see him again. A wave of sadness and regret overwhelmed her at that realisation.

'So, Gina,' he said now, reclaiming her attention. 'We were going to discuss why you are here.'

Nervousness gripped her. 'Yes, we were.'

'Why now? Why this beach? You cannot see it from the road, so how did you know it was here?' he pressed, and although his voice was warm, the challenge was unmistakable.

'I was looking for the rock called Neptune's Spear. When there was no reply at the villa, I decided to wait in case someone came home so I could talk to them. The temptation to go down to the beach and see if I had the right place was too much to resist. I had no idea you were down there swimming,' she explained, meeting his gaze, seeing a mix of curiosity and wariness in his eyes.

He regarded her for a long moment in silence. 'How did you know of the rock? Why is it that you wish to contact the owner of this villa?'

'It's a long story. A personal one.' She hesitated, wondering how to handle the situation. 'And it's not really mine to tell.'

'Then whose is it? You said you were here on Elba with someone?' he queried, his expression guarded.

'My grandmother.'

Surprise replaced the suspicion in his voice. 'Your *grandmother*?'

'Yes.' What had he been expecting her to say? And had she imagined that flash of relief that had crossed his face? It had happened too quickly for her to be certain. Pushing aside fanciful notions, she took a deep breath. 'Nonna Maria is Italian. Elba, and the beach at Neptune's Spear in particular, are special to her. She was here fifty years ago, and it has been her dream to come back.'

Interest sparked in his eyes. 'Fifty years? And she has not returned in all that time?'

'No. It wasn't possible for her to do so...for several reasons.' Gina spoke with caution, not wanting to reveal the sorry state of their finances. Nor did she wish to confide in anyone but the owner—the only one with the power to help them and grant their wish—the reason why they had made this important trip now.

'So what happened fifty years ago that means so much to her?' Seb probed, and she knew she would have to explain further.

'Nonna Maria was nineteen. She lived in Siena with her family, who took an annual holiday on Elba,' she began, warming to the story as Seb gave her his full attention. 'Matthew McNaught was a twenty-one-year-old ship's engineer. He was enjoying a few days off on the island with some friends while their vessel was under repair in port on the mainland. Both Maria and Matthew escaped for some time alone...and they met and fell in love on the beach by Neptune's rock.'

Seb's eyebrows rose in surprise. 'This beach?'

'Yes. My grandmother said no one lived here in those days.'

'What happened then?' he asked, making no comment about the villa.

'Matthew asked Maria to come to Scotland and marry him. Her family were rigidly opposed to the match, and demanded Maria return to Siena with them.'

'And what did she choose?'

Caramel eyes looked deep into hers, and it took Gina a moment to find her voice. 'She chose Matthew.' Her voice was uneven and she cleared her throat. What was it about this man that affected her so? It had never happened to her before. Aware he was waiting for her to continue, she attempted to rid herself of her wayward thoughts. 'I know the estrangement from her family pained my grandmother—there was no reconciliation—but she never regretted her decision. That life-changing moment led to fifty years of love and togetherness, through good times and bad.'

'You're a romantic.' His smile held the same touch of cynicism as his voice.

'Not really.' Her own tone cooled in response to his attitude, and to the memories of how Malcolm had trampled on her ideals. 'I just know that it worked for my grandparents. I can't imagine how hard it was for Nonna Maria, ripped away from her family and the country she knew, beginning a new life in a foreign land, not speaking the language, with her new husband away at sea for months until he secured a job in Glasgow's shipyards. They survived. They loved each other and were happy.'

Her grandparents' story had been her lifelong fairytale, her dream…a dream she had squashed down when she had lost hope of finding the kind of love they had shared for herself. She'd grown up and headed out into the adult world with those childhood hopes intact, but she had discovered that she couldn't have everything. Malcolm had taught her that. She had been forced to make a choice between her own needs or those of her grandparents. There had been no choice. Since then her own desires had been in cold storage. She had never met anyone who had under-stood her, and what was important to her, and she had given up believing she would ever find a man who would be to her what Matthew had been to Maria.

'And your grandfather—he is not here with you?'

Seb's question cut through her thoughts, and she gasped as fresh pain seared through her.

'Gina?'

'No,' she managed, meeting his gaze, seeing the concern in his eyes. 'He died several months ago.'

She swallowed down the renewed welling of grief, startled when Seb reached out a hand, resting it on her forearm. 'I am sorry, *cara*.'

'Thank you.' Gina thought of her grandmother, lost without the man who had been husband, friend, lover and confidant for fifty years, and of her own broken heart at losing the grandfather she had loved so much. 'It's not been easy…especially for Nonna Maria. The enforced sep-aration has taken its toll on her. She needed to come here.'

Heat radiated out from the point where Seb's skin touched hers. She struggled to ignore it, to fight against an awareness that was at once overwhelming yet exciting and unexpected, as if some internal thaw was beginning to reawaken the sensuous woman she had hidden away. His fingers lingered a moment longer, and when they were withdrawn she let out a shaky breath, both relieved and dis-appointed, unnerved by what was happening to her.

'I want to meet your grandmother.'

Gina's eyes widened in surprise. 'You do? Why?'

'I would like to hear about her history with this place, to know what it is that brings her back and why she wants to contact the villa's owner.' He paused, his gaze turning enigmatic once more. 'Unless there is some reason you do not wish me to speak with her?'

Gina realised this was a test—that Seb didn't yet believe her. Why was he so sceptical? What did he imagine she was doing here? For her grandmother's sake she had to convince him she was telling the truth.

'Not at all. I am sure Nonna will be delighted to talk to you. My concern is not to raise the hopes of a fragile old woman only to dash them if you then withhold your help,' she finished, issuing a challenge and a warning of her own.

'Gina—'

'I came alone today because, whilst Nonna's spirit may be strong, she is too frail for all the walking and waiting around. The journey from Scotland was tough on her,' she pressed on, ignoring the note of chastisement in his tone, unable to mask the protectiveness she felt for her grandmother. 'I don't want her upset—' She broke off and bit her lip, trying to rein in a sudden rush of emotion. 'We only have a few days here, and I want to make her happy.'

To her surprise, Seb's hands captured hers. 'I can promise you, Gina, that I will listen to what your grandmother has to say, and I will do all in my power to help her fulfil her wishes.'

'All right.' She couldn't say why, but she believed him. Relief flooded through her at the realisation she might not have failed her grandparents after all. 'Thank you.'

Gina wished she could excuse the unsteadiness of her voice and the rush of relief at Seb's guarantee, but she knew it was more due to the effect of his touch. Her skin was tingling, her heart racing. She was in real trouble. Her gaze clashed with his once more and she saw the speculation in his eyes—but also the answering heat and flare of masculine interest.

This kind of instant desire and feminine recognition was new to her. She was impossibly attracted to Seb. But she was only on Elba for a short time, and—more to the point—this trip was all about her grandmother, not herself. The last thing she should be thinking about was a man! Yet she couldn't prevent the rush of inner excitement that came with feeling like an attractive woman after a long spell in the dating wilderness.

'You will allow me to show you and your grandmother some Elban hospitality?' Seb asked now, his thumb tracing a tantalising caress across her palm.

'I don't know.'

Gina felt ridiculously flustered. She couldn't think when he touched her. Bemused at the speed of what was happening between them, she withdrew her hand from his. Her resolve was shaky, and it crumbled further under the warm appeal in his slumberous gaze. A short time in this man's company and she felt like a giddy teenager.

'Let me take you both to dinner,' he continued, his voice persuasive. 'We can talk more about your reasons for being here, and how I might help your grandmother.'

Gina wavered. It was important that this trip was a success, and Seb had played the one card guaranteed to make her weaken. This man could be all that stood between them and the agreement they needed to complete their mission on Elba.

'I'll have to ask Nonna Maria.'

'Of course.'

'In fact, I ought to go now.' Feeling an urgent need to remove herself from the temptation of Seb before she lost her head and did something crazy, Gina rose to her feet and picked up her bag. 'I don't like to leave her alone for too long, and she will be anxious for news.'

Something flickered across his face, but he masked it swiftly before she could assess what he was thinking. 'I shall escort you back. Then I can meet her and ask her myself.'

'You don't have to do that,' she protested, concerned at spending more time in his company before she had reinforced her defences, exerted some control over her wayward hormones and given herself a stern talking-to.

'Perhaps not…' He stood, his hand once more resting at the small of her back, sending new shivers along her spine as he guided her across the terrace. 'But I would like to.'

Again there was that edge in his voice. He might find

her attractive, but he was still unsure whether or not to believe her story. She didn't understand his misgivings, but the fact that he had them at all could affect the outcome for her grandmother. She had to do all she could to keep him on side—even if it did mean walking on dangerous ground herself. He only had to look at her or touch her and her common sense evaporated.

'All right.'

Before she knew it, he had taken a bike from the garage, she had told him where she was staying, and they were cycling west towards the village. Conscious of him every yard of the way, she wondered what her grandmother would have to say when she brought Seb home.

Gina couldn't help but feel nervous. This man was a stranger. A handsome and charismatic one—one who attracted and excited her like no other—but still a stranger. And now he had the power to make or break her grandmother's heart.

Would he help them?

Or would they be returning to Scotland disappointed?

CHAPTER THREE

As HE showered, Seb thought back over the afternoon. Maria had enchanted him from the first moment he had met her. Much like her granddaughter…but in a very different way.

For someone who usually remained detached, he had been deeply moved by Maria's story, and fascinated by her memories of the part of Elba he knew so well. The love and affection between her and Gina had been evident in every word and look, and although neither had yet revealed the reason why they wanted to contact the owners of the villa, his doubts about their genuineness were fading. Just listening to Maria talk had confirmed how important it was for her to be on Elba. Despite the emotional and physical upheaval of the trip for someone of her age, it was a final pilgrimage she obviously needed to complete. He wanted to help Maria—and to learn more about Gina. The opportunity to begin that process had presented itself when Maria had accepted his invitation to take them both to dinner.

Knotting a towel around his waist, he sat on his bed and reached for the phone to call his cousin. Now thirty-three, he and Rico were only a few months apart in age, although their early upbringing had been very different. Rico was more outgoing, more trusting, but as a top allergist and immunologist, with his own successful clinic, he was just as dedicated to his career in medicine.

Rico answered promptly, and Seb filled him in on Maria's story and the connection to the family villa.

'You're lucky that Mamma is away on business with the charity, or she would be over there in a flash to investigate,' Rico suggested with wry amusement.

Lovely as Zia Sofia was, Seb was relieved she was not around to interfere. He wanted to handle this situation on his own. Which brought him to his reason for calling his cousin. 'Why does the name Strathlochan mean something to me?'

'It's the county town near the village where Nic di Angelis lives,' Rico reminded him. 'I worked with him in Milan a few years ago—and I went over to Scotland for the wedding when he married his GP partner, Hannah.'

'How strange.'

'Is that where these women are from?' Rico asked, sounding as surprised at the coincidence as he was.

'They moved there from Glasgow. Until a few days ago Gina worked in the A and E department at Strathlochan Hospital.' Seb hesitated a moment. 'Are you still in touch with Nic? Would you be able to make some discreet enquiries for me?'

'Tell me what you need and I'll talk to him.'

'Thanks, Rico. I want to make certain everything is above board.' He paused, still feeling the flicker of guilt he had experienced when Gina had introduced him to her grandmother as the caretaker. 'At the moment they don't know who I am, or what my connection is to the villa.'

There was a long pause. 'Seb, what are you doing?'

'I need to be sure there are no ulterior motives. I've said I'll do what I can to help when I know what it is Maria wants,' he pressed on, ignoring the warning in his cousin's voice.

'I'll check things out with Nic, but my hunch is the same as yours. These women are genuine.' Rico was silent a moment, and his voice was solemn when he spoke again. 'I know what Antonella did to you, that it's made you cautious and untrusting. And I know how difficult things have been with the press intrusion. But Maria and Gina are not media people out to get you. Don't you think you should tell them the truth?'

Sighing, Seb leaned back against the pillows and closed his eyes. He didn't want to think about Antonella and her deception. Or the press. Or his so-called celebrity status. How could he explain to Rico that he had enjoyed being treated as an ordinary person? He didn't want Gina and Maria to judge him on his name or his money.

'I'll tell them when the time is right.'

'On your head be it.' His cousin's disagreement at the decision was plain. 'Before I go, you need to know there are still reporters sniffing around your apartment. A couple have been here, to the clinic, and Papà took no nonsense from one who went to the house.'

Seb ran the fingers of one of his now less able hands across his brow, biting back his annoyance at the way the press were hounding his family. 'I'm sorry.'

'It's fine. I just wanted to fill you in on the official line.'

'And that is?'

Rico chuckled. 'That you have gone overseas. Well, it is kind of true, no?'

'Thanks.'

'No problem, *cugino*. Hang in there. I'll be in touch. Enjoy your dinner tonight with the lovely ladies…and tell them you're not the caretaker.'

Seb set down the phone and rose to dress, trying to ignore Rico's advice. Instead, he thought of the evening ahead. He had been surprised to discover Gina and Maria sharing a small room in a cheap bed and breakfast—but, combined with a few other clues, he had guessed that money was tight and it had been a financial struggle for them to come to Elba. Despite the luxuries his career had brought him, he had not forgotten what it was like to live from hand to mouth, to be thrifty, to go without. As he tended to wear casual clothes on the island, he ignored the handful of designer suits hanging in his wardrobe and dressed down, wanting to put them at ease.

Having learned that they both enjoyed seafood, he had chosen a restaurant that was inexpensive and friendly but had a reputation for excellent food. He'd not been there before, and he hoped no one would recognise him—or, if they did, that they would be discreet. He had not forgotten Rico's warning, but he was not yet ready to reveal his true identity to Maria and Gina.

Gina. Anticipation gripped him at the thought of seeing her again. He had never felt such an instant attraction to a woman before. She was only here for a short time, so it would be crazy to act on the searing desire that charged through him whenever he was near her. But, fool that he was, whatever the consequences, he couldn't keep away.

Picking up the keys to the basic runabout his uncle kept for driving on the island, he headed for the door, tension and expectation tightening inside him. It was time. Time to meet Maria again. Time to be with Gina.

Gina dressed for the evening, conscious of the fact that she was taking far more care over her appearance than she had in ages. It was a long time since she had felt feminine and desired—just as long since she had spent any time thinking about a man. But meeting Seb this afternoon, experiencing an attraction the depth of which she had never known before, made her feel as if she was awakening from a long slumber. A self-imposed hibernation sparked when Malcolm had delivered his ultimatum. She had made her decision then and had stuck to it, never feeling tempted... until now.

She thought of her grandmother's words of concern that she had put her life on hold. She didn't begrudge a moment of the time she had spent caring for her grandparents, but between them and the pressures of work there had been little time for an active social life. She saw her girlfriends when their shifts allowed, but she had neither the time nor the interest in dating, would never take the risk of someone trying to come between her and her family again. It had never crossed her mind before today just how long it had been since she had given any thought to her own needs as a woman.

Seb was the sexiest, most compelling man she had ever met. And potentially the most dangerous to her resolve. Just being with him brought long-forgotten wants bubbling to the surface, and she tried to remind herself for the ump-teenth time that she had to continue to set her own wishes aside and remember that this trip was all about her grand-mother. She couldn't risk letting her desire for a man jeop-ardise that. On the other hand, Seb could be the one to help them gain the villa-owner's permission for what they had come to Elba to do. They needed him. She very much feared she needed him in a very different way.

After moisturising her skin following a bath, she applied some mascara to accentuate her eyes and a touch of colour to her lips. Leaving her hair loose, she dabbed some vanilla-scented perfume on her pulse-points and behind her ears, then stepped back to take one last look at her reflec-tion in the mirror. Not knowing where Seb might be taking them she'd put on the best dress she had brought with her. It had capped sleeves and a scooped neckline, which revealed rather a lot of her generous cleavage, while the rich red fabric clung to her curves before fanning out at the hips, the skirt rippling to her knees. Flat shoes, a black wool wrap and her bag completed the outfit. She was ready. If only she didn't feel so nervous. Her heart scampered fit to burst, and a shiver of delicious anticipation tingled down her spine—warnings, if she needed any more, of just how fast and how deep she was falling for this man.

'*Che bellezza!* How lovely you look,' her grandmother praised with a delighted clap of her hands as Gina stepped out of the tiny bathroom and into the bedroom they shared.

'Thank you.'

'Seb will be a man much envied tonight.'

Gina flushed at the gentle teasing. 'He is doing this to help you,' she reminded her, trying to push away her own edgy excitement at the thought of seeing him again.

'I believe his reasons are much more basic. You are as attracted to him as he is to you,' her grandmother stated with uncanny perception.

'We're only here for a few days—' Gina struggled to keep reminding herself of that fact '—and seeing to your needs is all that matters.'

Her grandmother waved her hand dismissively. 'Nonsense, *ragazza mia.*'

'Nonna—'

'I cannot stop caring and worrying, Gina. Despite your protests, I know you have given up so much for your grandfather and me. We never intended to restrict your life by coming to live with you.'

'You haven't,' Gina protested, knowing for the first time that it was not entirely the truth.

Her grandmother took one of her hands in both of hers. 'You are a beautiful woman, but I think you have forgotten this. Today, for the first time, I can see you blossoming again, and it pleases me more than I can say.'

'We are here for a reason—'

'Which does not mean you should not enjoy yourself also,' her grandmother interrupted. 'Have some fun, enjoy the romance. Who knows where the attraction you and Seb share might take you?'

'Nonna…' Her protest died as confusion racked her. Could she really indulge in a holiday romance? 'I don't know.'

'Live your life, *ragazza mia.* Had I listened to all the doubts, I would not have had my special lifetime with your grandfather. I would always want you to follow your heart,' her grandmother insisted, the expression in her hazel eyes serious.

But could she trust her heart? Gina worried. How

could she yearn for Seb after such a short time? Was it just lust? Did that even matter? They were both adults. If they were both free...

'I've only just met him, Nonna. We live in different countries. How can I know?'

'You say this to *me*?' Tutting, her grandmother shook her head. 'I knew in that first instant when I met Matthew McNaught. Time means nothing, Gina...not when it is right. When you meet your soul mate, you *know*. Do not put obstacles in the way. Do not let concern for me sway you. I would never want that. Your happiness is my happiness. Do not be afraid to go for what you want.'

Tears stung her eyes as she absorbed her grandmother's advice—what was tantamount to her blessing to explore the incredible connection she had felt with Seb from the instant she had seen him. But she couldn't help but be cautious. Nothing like this had ever happened to her before. She had never met anyone like Seb, had never reacted to anyone the way she did to him.

'I like Seb, Gina,' her grandmother continued, drawing her from her thoughts. 'I have always had good instincts about people. I believe we can trust him. We must confide in him our reasons for being here.'

Fresh concern welled inside her. 'Are you sure? We need the permission of the villa's owner.'

'Maybe not. Seb has already said they will not return to Elba for some time. We don't have time. I need to do this, *ragazza mia*, and I trust Seb to help us.'

Before she could formulate a reply, or gather her thoughts together, there was a knock at the door. Her wayward heart skittered alarmingly, and a tremor ran through her, a whole flight of butterflies fluttering inside her.

Her grandmother cupped her cheek, understanding behind her smile. 'Open the door, Gina. And don't shut the woman you truly are away again. What will be will be.'

Filled with a mix of confusion and excitement, Gina

crossed the room, her hand shaking as she turned the handle. Then the breath locked in her lungs and her heart threatened to stop beating altogether before rampaging on again at an alarming rate. And all because Seb stood there, looking even more amazing than she remembered him. Dressed in dark grey trousers and matching short-sleeved shirt, he was dangerously, deliciously handsome. Her gaze clashed with his. Caramel eyes held warmth, appreciation, and a smouldering awareness that made her burn and threatened to strip away any remaining shred of common sense or resistance. And then he smiled, a slow, private smile that turned her insides molten.

'Good evening, Gina,' he greeted her in English. The smoky, accented voice caused her knees to weaken further. A blush tinged her cheeks as his sultry gaze made a leisurely journey over her, lingering at her chest, an approving gleam in his eyes. 'You look stunning.'

'Thank you.'

Flustered, she stepped back and allowed Seb into the room, thankful when he turned his attention to her grandmother. She needed a couple of moments to recover her composure.

'Maria, it is lovely to see you again,' he said, with the easy smile and smooth charm that appeared so natural to him. He held out a bunch of flowers. 'These are for you, *cara*. Signora Mancini is finding a vase to put them in.'

'They are beautiful. Thank you so much!'

Gina saw the flush of pleasure warm her grandmother's cheeks and was grateful for Seb's thoughtfulness.

'*Prego*. You are welcome.' Turning, he closed the distance between them and held out a single, fragrant bloom—a pure white rose. 'For you, Gina.'

She couldn't halt her own blush, nor the welling of emotion at the simple but meaningful gesture. 'Thank you,' she murmured, her voice unusually husky. She had forgotten what it was like to be romanced, she thought, breathing in the delicious scent of the perfect flower before setting it next to her grandmother's bouquet.

He held her gaze for a long moment, but glanced away, his attention sharpening as her grandmother smothered another couple of coughs. Her unease returning, Gina stepped forward.

'Are you all right, Nonna?'

'I am fine. Just tired. If you don't mind, I shall decline dinner this evening,' she added, shocking Gina to silence. 'Signora Mancini and I have become good friends. She is making me her special recipe ravioli, and then we are going to play a game of chess before I have an early night. You must go and have fun, Gina. Do not always allow me to slow you down. This is your holiday, too.'

'But...'

'Go, *ragazza mia*. Please. You can explain to Seb what is needed.'

Outwitted, Gina hesitated again and glanced at Seb. She had the most terrible feeling her grandmother was match-making in the most unsubtle way. Part of her yearned to spend some time with Seb, but the rest of her was reluctant to leave her grandmother, her anxiety increasing over the cough she had been developing in the last couple of days.

'If you are sure that is what you want, Maria, then I will be honoured to escort Gina for the evening and bring her safely home again,' he reassured her, taking a notebook from his pocket and tearing out a piece of paper. 'I will write down the name and number of the restaurant, and of my mobile phone, then you or Signora Mancini can contact us at any time if necessary.' He turned to glance at her. 'Is that all right with you, Gina?'

'OK.'

Heat flashed in his eyes at her whispered reply. All her defences were stripped away. She was grateful for his understanding, his care with her grandmother, and for his consideration of her own feelings. The decision made, the three of them walked to the front hall, where Signora Mancini waited, assuring them again that all would be well.

'Remember what I said, *ragazza mia*,' her grandmother whispered as she hugged her. 'Think of yourself for a change. And trust Seb with our request. Have faith.'

Then Gina found herself outside. Alone with Seb.

'You don't have to do this,' she began, offering him a way out even as he took her hand and led her towards the small Fiat that was parked at the roadside. 'It wasn't the arrangement.'

'Maybe not. And I truly would have enjoyed Maria's company. But I cannot say I am sorry to have you to myself.'

Taking a deep breath, she looked at him, unable to doubt his sincerity. 'If you're sure,' she murmured, realising how close they were as she breathed in the subtle woodsy scent of him.

'I am very sure, Gina.'

The certainty in his voice matched the desire in his eyes and sent a fresh tingle down her spine. The charge of electricity between them was unmistakable, the attraction intense, scary, exhilarating. She waited until she was settled in the car and Seb was walking round the other side before she drew in a few deep, steadying breaths.

At just twenty-eight kilometres long and nineteen kilometres at the widest point, the island was compact, and they did not have far to travel.

'Where are we going?' Gina asked, the gathering dusk masking the scenery of a part of the island she had not yet seen.

'I booked a table at a small seafront restaurant in Marciana Marina.' Seb smiled across at her. 'It's a picturesque fishing harbour, with a Pisan watchtower overlooking the shingle beach. The town is ancient, the smallest *comune* in Tuscany, and although an elegant resort is growing, the old quarter of the village—Cotone—is being carefully maintained.'

'It must be wonderful to live here. I've read so much about the island and its fascinating history. Has Elba always been home for you?'

'No.'

Surprised at the shortness of his reply, she glanced at him out of the corner of her eye. But before she could question him further they had reached the town, situated at the end of a valley, and Seb was parking the car. He came round to open the door for her, all smiles again.

'All right?' She nodded, distracted from her moment of uneasiness by the sights around her. Seb took her hand again, his touch increasing her awareness and firing her blood. 'Come, Gina, The restaurant isn't far.'

They walked a short way along the promenade before they came to an intimate-looking restaurant tucked away from the busy bars and tourist trinket shops. The smiling owner led them through the main dining area to a secluded terrace, settling them at a table where the muted lighting created a romantic atmosphere. The ambience was height-ened by the clarity of the evening, the play of moonlight across the gently undulating waters, and the expanse of stars in the darkening sky.

'It's lovely,' she sighed, her gaze taking everything in before switching back to look at Seb. 'Have you been here before?'

He shook his head. 'A friend recommended it. Let us study the menu. What would you like?'

Despite the attraction zinging between them, Seb made her feel comfortable as they discussed the mouthwatering choices available. Eating out was a rare treat for her these days, and she considered all the dishes with enthusiasm, finding an array of exciting ingredients she would never have at home.

'I think I'll have the red mullet cooked with tomatoes, garlic and parsley,' she decided, embarrassed when her tummy gave an audible rumble in hungry anticipation.

'I think that is my sign to hurry and order,' Seb teased, selecting the shellfish risotto for himself and handing the menus back to the discreet waiter. 'What would you like to drink, Gina? You must try an Elban wine while you are here.'

'What would you recommend?'

She found herself distracted by the movement of his lips as he told her about the local wines, the husky cadence of his voice washing over her, warming her. He really was the most incredibly handsome man. All this could so easily go to her head...being wined, dined and charmed after so long in dating limbo. She—

'Gina?'

'Sorry?' A blush tinged her cheeks as she shook off her mental meanderings and noticed Seb watching her with an amused smile. 'What did you say?'

'Perhaps you will trust me to choose the wine for you?' he suggested, and she realised she had been so busy looking at him that she hadn't taken in a word he had said.

She cleared her throat. 'Yes, please do.'

Usually she would have a glass of rosé Lambrusco with her friends while sharing a pizza, but she was happy to take Seb's advice, listening as he gave the order for a local dry white wine for her. He, she noted, kept to mineral water.

'Your grandmother is a delightful lady,' Seb praised as they enjoyed some antipasti while waiting for their main courses to arrive.

Gina smiled with affection. 'She is.'

'You are very close.'

'Yes. And with my grandfather, too,' she agreed at his observation.

'I am sorry, Gina.' His fingertips brushed her bare arm and she shivered in reaction to the empathetic touch. 'You must miss him very much.'

'I do. I still find it hard to believe he's gone. It's been worse for Nonna, of course.'

Seb's smile was gentle. 'It is good that you have each other.'

'Thank you.' She felt a moment of real closeness with him, feeling that he truly understood the bonds of family—unlike Malcolm.

'Tell me about Strathlochan,' he invited as their plates of aromatic food arrived. 'You enjoy it there?'

'Very much so. After growing up in quite a rough part of Glasgow, it was like paradise to find myself surrounded by lochs, hills and forests,' she explained with a smile. 'It's a beautiful region, and a great place to live. Although the town is growing, it has kept the community feel.'

Whether it was the wine, or the way Seb had of making her feel interesting and important, Gina found herself revealing far more about herself than she had intended. He was attentive, warm, funny and intelligent—and he made her feel special, the only person who mattered to him. It was a heady experience, and she felt the hidden woman she had buried inside coming back to life.

As they lingered over the delicious meal, they talked about books and music, films and politics, finding much in common and a few things they disagreed about, enjoying a good-natured teasing debate. She hadn't laughed so much in ages, Gina realised, taking a sip of her delicious wine, or felt so appreciated as a woman. When Seb encouraged her to talk more about the things that mattered to her, she told him about her grandmother, her home, her nursing and her best friends…quiet, studious nurse Holly Tait, and over-achieving, single-minded GP Ruth Baxter.

'Ruth is keeping an eye on Montgomery while we're away.'

'Montgomery?' Seb questioned, and Gina couldn't help chuckling at his wary uncertainty.

'My black Labrador.'

A flicker of relief crossed his expression. 'You have a dog?'

'I do. I love animals. I'd have a whole menagerie if I had the time and space.' And the money, she added silently. 'Monty was found abandoned at six months old, and we were delighted to give him a home. He's lovely—a year old now, and wonderful company for Nonna when I am at work. Like me, she's a big fan of old films, and we chose the name because she was reading a biography of Montgomery Clift at the time. Nonna said he was dark, handsome and had a flawed upbringing—like his namesake.'

Smiling, Seb nodded. 'And you say you start a new job when you go home?'

'Yes.' Finishing her meal, she set down her knife and fork. 'I'll be working at Strathlochan's new multi-purpose drop-in centre. I enjoyed the trauma work, but there was a lot of pressure and long shifts. I want more regular hours so I can care for Nonna. I could have gone to a higher grade at the hospital, but it would have meant I lost the hands-on work with patients, and that's what the job is all about for me. You have to do what makes you happy and maintain your principles, don't you?'

Seb remained silent. Unlike Gina, he hadn't held firm, but had given in to the lures and inducements to go against all he had believed in. The realisation that he should have stayed true to himself and his roots was sobering. He thought of Rico's advice to tell Gina who he was, but after listening to her speak with such dedication he feared she would think less of him for what he had been and had done.

'Goodness!' she exclaimed with embarrassment as the silence between them lengthened. 'I've been very boring, talking so much about myself.'

'You could never be boring.' He watched her thoughtfully for a moment. 'You speak with such loyalty and love about your family, your friends and your work. But what of you, Gina?'

'Me?'

She looked surprised, as if she didn't think she mattered, confirming his suspicions that she put everyone else before herself. 'Yes. When is Gina time? What do *you* want? What are *your* dreams?'

'I don't know.' She frowned, her fingers fussing with the stem of her glass. 'It's a long time since I've thought about it,' she admitted then, her gaze lifting to reveal the confusion in dark eyes. 'I suppose I've defined myself for so long by family and work. They're important to me.'

He reached out and took her hand in his, relishing being able to touch her again, enjoying the feel of her soft skin against his own. 'As they should be. There is nothing wrong with that. But you are important, too. You should be happy, content, fulfilled.'

As he said the words, meaning them, it dawned on him that they applied equally to his own life. When had he bothered about his own needs? He'd thrown his whole self into his career, needing to succeed, covering up for the fact that it no longer brought him the satisfaction it once had…not since the hospital board had cajoled him into cutting back on the reconstructive work he did for those with birth defects or accident injuries in favour of the celebrity nip/tuck work that brought money and kudos for the hospital as well as himself. It was only now, talking with Gina, that he'd really opened his eyes and his mind to that. It gave him much more to think about regarding the future direction of his life.

'And is there a man waiting impatiently for your return to Scotland?' he asked, his voice less steady than he wanted. But he needed to know.

Spending this time with Gina had reinforced his desire for her, and confirmed how much he liked her as a person. He couldn't remember when he had last enjoyed himself so much, nor when he had been so interested and entertained talking with a woman—one who was not fixated on her appearance, her quest for fame, or what his money and contacts could do for her.

'There's no one,' Gina replied, lifting an anxious weight from his chest. 'I—'

Still holding her hand, he stroked her wrist, feeling the acceleration of her pulse. 'Tell me.'

'I've not really dated in a while,' she admitted, becoming colour staining her cheeks.

'Why not?' Were the men in Scotland blind? 'How long is "a while"?'

She shrugged, her gaze sliding from his. 'About four years.'

'Four years?' he repeated, staggered at the information.

'I guess I've been so busy caring for my grandparents and doing my job. There was someone, but…'

'But?' he encouraged, seeing her frown, sensing this was important.

She paused, nibbling at her lower lip in a way that sparked a fire in his gut. 'My last relationship didn't survive my grandparents coming to live with me. I made a decision then about my priorities, and there hasn't really been the opportunity since.'

It wasn't hard to read between the lines. The man she had been dating at the time had been unwilling to share her attention, so Gina had devoted herself to the needs of others to such an extent that she had forgotten about her own. Seb admired her loyalty, her thoughtfulness. It made him like and desire her even more. But he wanted to help Gina remember just how much of a woman she was.

Before he could voice his thoughts, the waitress arrived and asked if they wanted dessert. Seb declined, ordering a coffee and chuckling at Gina's eagerness to sample the restaurant's home-made ice cream. Reluctantly, he relinquished her hand.

Midway through savouring her sweet treat, she glanced up, the expression on her face making him smile again. She looked self-conscious, but wryly amused.

'I'm being a pig, aren't I?' she bemoaned.

'Not at all. Honestly. It's a pleasure to dine with someone who enjoys their food and has an appreciation for what they are eating…and for the chef who prepared it.'

He thought of women like Lidia, taken to the finest restaurants, who made a fuss over every course, who picked at the food and refused to touch more than a few salad leaves. They cared little about the wastefulness, thought nothing of those who had less than they did, nor gave a mind to the people who had worked hard to deliver the food. Their selfishness and unnatural thinness were unattractive. Gina, on the other hand, was infinitely more sexy and enticing and head-turning for her true feminine curves. And she was natural, honest, completely uninterested in artificiality. It was wonderfully refreshing.

Seb watched her as she finished off her dessert, finding himself aroused by her almost sensual enjoyment of the taste and texture of what she was eating. She wasn't classically beautiful, and bore none of the carefully manufactured polish and sophistication of his rich patients, or the women who had vied—usually unsuccessfully—for his attention. But it was Gina's very naturalness that appealed to him and brought home how fake and unattractive all those other women were. Gina's was an inner beauty. Here was a woman who was comfortable with herself and who was not trying to impress or be something or someone else. His desire for her intensified.

There had been a few women in his past. He had been attracted to Antonella, but any interest had died when he had discovered she was an undercover reporter doing a kiss-and-tell story on him. That had hurt. He had never let anyone into his life again. There had been other women who wanted to be seen with him to further their own careers, to get their pictures in the papers, their names known. They were never interested in him as a person. His career had been pressured and time-consuming, the most important thing to him, and he'd had no time for a relationship.

Gina was the kind of woman he would once have run away from at full speed, but now his feet were planted firmly on the ground and weren't moving. Despite his initial caution, he'd known from the first that Gina was different. He had never been so instantly drawn to a woman. Not just her looks, but everything about her—her manner, her humour, her quiet intelligence, her sense of fun, her caring nature. Her loyal affection for her friends and the fact that she gave so much of herself to her grandmother said a lot about her, too.

He wanted to spend time with her—wanted to know everything about her. And he most definitely wanted to make love to her. He sensed hidden passions, an untapped sensuality he yearned to explore—a side of her she freely admitted she had selflessly restricted due to her responsibilities at home. While she was here on Elba he hoped to encourage the real Gina out to play.

CHAPTER FOUR

SEB was sorry when it was time for them to leave the restaurant. He had hoped to spend longer with Gina, to stroll along the harbour front, fringed with tamarisks, or go back to the villa and talk some more. But he knew she was anxious to return and check on Maria.

'You're sure you don't mind?' she asked as he called for the bill, although her relief was clear, too.

'Of course not.' Her sense of family and her thoughtfulness for others were two of the many things he admired so much about her. 'I understand.' He watched as she opened her bag and took out her purse. 'Gina, what are you doing?'

'Paying my share,' she stated, her eyes widening as he reached out and closed his hand over hers.

'Absolutely not.'

Doubt registered, and she hesitated. 'It's what I do at home,' she explained, and he wondered at the kind of men she had dated in the past.

'It's not what *I* do when I ask a woman to dine with me.' He stroked the back of his fingers down the smooth perfection of her cheek, touched by her generosity. 'Please, this is my treat.'

'OK.'

He drew her hand to his mouth, pressing a kiss to her palm, hearing her breath hitch. 'Thank you, Gina.'

The question of the bill settled, they left the restaurant and drove back to the hamlet in which Signora Mancini's house was situated. While he had enjoyed learning more about Gina, he realised that they had still not discussed the purpose of her and Maria's visit to Elba.

'Tell me more about your grandmother's wish, and this request she wants to make of the villa's owner,' he suggested, glancing at Gina and noting the way she nervously toyed with the hem of her wrap. 'She is hoping to revisit the beach?'

'Yes.' A deep sigh escaped her. 'That was the plan.'

'You realise there is no way Maria is going to be able to use the cliff steps?'

'I know. It was obvious from the first moment I saw them,' she admitted with resignation, and he regretted dampening her spirits.

All too soon they arrived outside the bed and breakfast. He walked round and opened the car door for Gina. Taking her hand, needing to touch her, to keep her close, he went up the path towards the open veranda that ran along the front of the building. He halted at the top of the half dozen shallow wooden stairs so they could have some privacy and talk.

'Is there any other way down the cliff to the beach?' she asked now, hope in her voice.

'No. I'm afraid not.'

Her shoulders slumped in apparent defeat. 'I guess that's it, then.'

He turned her to face him, the light from the porch combining with the moonlight to cast a gentle glow over her skin, illuminating her pensive expression. 'Tell me, Gina. Trust me. What is so important?'

'My grandparents made a vow to each other...and I promised to help.'

'Go on,' he encouraged when she paused, still puzzled by her reticence.

'The place where they met was always special to them.'

He knew this, but he waited for her to get to the point in her own time. Ducking her head to avoid his gaze, she drew her wrap more tightly around her shoulders, and he stepped closer, rubbing his hands lightly up and down her arms.

'Nonna didn't want to tell anyone, to ask anyone but the owner, because...' Again she paused, taking a deep breath before she rushed out the final words. 'I'm not sure it's legal.'

'Not legal?' For a moment Seb froze. 'What do you mean?'

'Nonna promised she would scatter my grandfather's ashes on the spot where they first met. I did some research and, while the law banning the practice in Italy changed some years ago, you need official permission, and some places still don't allow it. We don't have a permit. It isn't something we could do without asking the people who own the beach, and Nonna doesn't want anyone to get into trouble for helping her.' She sucked in another breath, her voice little more than a whisper. 'She wants me to bring her ashes here, too...when the time comes.'

He heard the wobble in her voice, knew how much her grandparents meant to her and how hard this must be for her. Taking her in his arms, he held her close, knowing he would do anything he could to make her happy and help her deliver on her promises. Cradling her against him, he buried his face in the thick lustrous waves of her glorious hair, breathing in the subtle and arousing scent he was coming to know as uniquely Gina.

'We can do it, *tesoro*,' he told her, turning the possibilities over in his mind.

'But how? You said yourself there is no way Nonna can make it down the steps.'

'That is true,' he agreed, but an idea had taken root. 'I have another plan.'

He allowed her to draw back enough to meet his gaze, and saw the dawn of cautious expectation in her dark eyes. 'You do? What is it?'

'We can take Maria to the cove by sea. I have a friend who will help us. He has a boat he uses for tourist trips and to take out divers. We can both go with her to keep her safe. It can be done, Gina. If Maria wishes.'

'But what about the owner of the villa? And the permit? Time is running out,' she fretted, continuing to talk around the fingertips he'd touched to her lips to silence her. 'What is their name?'

It would do no harm to tell her that much. 'The family's name is Linardi. I know them well enough to be certain that they would be happy to help you. I promise you it will be all right.'

'You're positive?'

'One hundred per cent,' he stated, seeing tears spiking her lashes.

'Thank you.'

Taking him by surprise, she threw her arms around him in a spontaneous hug and pressed an all-too-quick kiss to his startled mouth. Instinctively his arms tightened around her, holding her close, but she was pulling back before he had the chance to savour or extend the kiss.

'Sorry about that,' she murmured, sounding shaken, her voice uneven.

'I'm not.' He saw the flame of awareness in her eyes, and something else she could not hide…a yearning need that matched his own. Smiling, he dropped his gaze to her luscious lips. 'Let's try it again. Together this time.'

Without giving either of them a chance to reconsider, he leaned in and touched his mouth to hers, swept along on a tide of passion more immediate and intense than he had ever known. At once he was engulfed in her heat, her sweetness, the scent of vanilla and woman exciting and ensnaring him. She moaned softly, her lips opening under his. He made full use of the invitation, startled by the way the desire between them flared out of control in an instant. That had never happened to him before. He had never lost control, never absorbed himself in a woman, yet just kissing Gina stripped away all his reserve, exposing his base instincts, his raw need. Her taste, her scent, the feel of her soft curves against him, drove him wild.

Madre del Dio! Another few moments and he would forget himself, forget where they were, and take this whirlwind to its inevitable conclusion. He couldn't do that. Not here. Not now. When the time came—as he hoped it would—he wanted Gina in his bed, where he could take his time and spend all night savouring her, loving her as she deserved. Until this inexplicable storm of desire spent itself. And if it didn't? He tried to ignore the inner voice telling him that the passion between them would only burn hotter and hotter. Gina only had a few more days on Elba. He wanted to make the most of them.

Breaking the kiss, he looked at her, lips plump and rosy from his kiss, her body shaking, her arousal evident in the flush of colour staining her cheeks, dark brown eyes almost black with passion.

'Perhaps we've both spent too long being serious and responsible,' he suggested, hearing the roughness in his own voice. With the fingertips of one hand, he explored the contours of her face, amazed anew at the softness of her skin. 'Together we will have some fun, yes? Take time to be carefree.'

'Seb…'

His name whispered from her parted lips. He groaned, unable to help himself as he returned his mouth to hers, sparking off another storm of passion. Gina kissed like an angel. Or maybe that should be a sorceress, given the way she had bewitched and beguiled him. He had lost his head from their first meeting on the beach.

Sweet mercy, the man could kiss.

Gina was carried away by the rush of desire charging through her. Seb's slow, deep kisses were consuming and heart-stoppingly sexy. She met and matched every demand…every stroke and glide as their tongues teased and tasted. The magic of Seb was awakening her from her slumber, making her aware for the first time in years of her own body, stirring long-ignored needs inside her. It was four years since she had been kissed, but she didn't remember it ever being like this! Every particle of her skin tingled, her nerves hummed, the blood sped through her veins. Inhaling his masculine scent, she felt drunk on him. She couldn't get close enough, and was oblivious to everything, focused solely on Seb and how incredible he made her feel.

When he drew back a second time they were both breathing raggedly, their hearts thudding in unison. She barely had time to think, much less gather her scattered senses, before he sank his hands in her hair, tilting her head so his mouth could trail a sensual path of fire down her throat and along her neck.

'Seb.' His name escaped on a whimper—appeal, not protest—and she tightened her hold on him, her legs like jelly, unable to support her much longer.

His breath was hot against her skin as his teeth nipped one earlobe before he salved the tiny sting with his tongue. 'You feel it too.'

'I do.' How could she deny his husky declaration? 'But I'm only here for a couple more days.'

'So were Maria and Matthew all those years ago. Don't you think we owe it to ourselves to see where this might go?'

Gina didn't know what to say. She had no idea what was happening between them, but meeting Seb had opened her eyes to the way she had disregarded her own wants. It had taken this man, in this place, to bring her back to life. No one else had ever affected her as Seb did, no one had kissed her as he did, or set her on fire with a single touch. Seb made her feel sensual, desirable, feminine, strong. She would never let anyone come between her and her grandmother, but Seb was no threat to her responsibilities at home. Here on this magical island, steeped in romance, could she indulge herself for a few days, free the woman within, the woman who had only come alive again for Seb?

'My grandmother…'

'I know. I want to spend time with you, but Maria is important, too,' he assured her, and his understanding, his care, his willingness to include her grandmother eased any lingering concern. 'Let me take you sightseeing tomorrow. Both of you. We can discuss with Maria how to put our plan into action.'

She felt overwhelmed, light-headed, wondering if she had the courage to take a risk and see where this mutual attraction took them. She looked into Seb's eyes, his intense expression almost melting her on the spot, and knew she had never wanted anyone or anything this much in her whole life.

'It would be a shame not to experience everything the island has to offer while you are here, Gina.'

She dragged in a steadying breath and tried not to get carried away by the sultry suggestion in his voice. 'I—'

'Tomorrow we will take Maria on a special outing, yes?'

'Yes.' The joy of being with him overrode any remaining fragment of common sense she still possessed. 'I'll talk to her in the morning.'

'I shall call for you after breakfast and learn of your decision.'

'Thank you. And for this evening,' she added, feeling melancholy at having to say goodnight. 'I've had a lovely time.'

'So have I.'

He took her hand, re-establishing the physical connection and re-stoking the passion inside her. That he felt it, too, was apparent by the heat burning in his eyes. A tremor rippled through her as he held her gaze, raising her hand to his mouth and pressing a tantalising kiss to the inside of her wrist, his tongue-tip stroking teasing circles on her skin. He only had to look at her, touch her, kiss her, and she was gone. Everything about him was so sensual, so intense, and yet he had a gentleness and inherent caring that made him even more appealing and impossible to resist.

His fingers combed through her hair again, as if he couldn't stop touching her, while under her own hands she felt the play of muscle across his back, firm, supple, exciting. It had been so long since she had felt wanted, desired…and she had *never* experienced this kind of physical and emotional connection with a man before.

'I should say goodnight,' he murmured, nibbling at her lower lip, which remained full and sensitised from his kisses.

'I suppose,' she whispered back, her fingertips skimming down his spine.

Neither of them let go. Neither moved back. Their gazes locked. Endless moments passed. Then Seb surrendered. Her lips parted in welcome, meeting his in another searing kiss. She had no idea what the future held, but she couldn't stop the onward rush of whatever was happening between them. Didn't *want* to stop it.

She moaned in protest when he began to pull back again. If only she never had to stop holding him, kissing him. 'Seb?'

'You must go indoors, *tesoro*.' His voice was uneven, thick with desire. 'Now—while I can still let you.'

She wanted to step back into his arms and throw caution to the wind, but Seb was opening the front door and encouraging her inside.

'Until the morning, Gina.' His fingers whispered across her cheek and down her throat to the hollow where her pulse beat a crazy tattoo. 'Dream of me…as I will of you.'

Gina had no idea how she forced her legs to move, but she found herself inside…alone. She sagged back against the door that separated them, breathless and trembling, one hand pressed to her chest. There was a long silence before Seb's footsteps carried him away, and she had to fight the urge to run after him and stop him from leaving.

She couldn't imagine how she would ever sleep. She was buzzing. The feel and taste of Seb lingered.

When she could force herself to move, she tiptoed along to the ground-floor room she shared with her grandmother. She couldn't wait to tell her the good news—that Seb was making plans to help them scatter Nonno Matthew's ashes in the villa's private cove near Neptune's Spear. For now she was thankful to find the older woman asleep, although she was restless, her breathing less regular than normal, stirring concern that all was not well.

Careful not to make a sound, Gina readied for bed and slipped beneath the light duvet. Her gaze lingered on the beautiful white rose Seb had brought her, which now sat on the table beside her bed in a narrow vase, courtesy of Signora Mancini. She leaned across and inhaled the scent, a smile on her face, her fingertips brushing the silky softness of the petals. Worry for her grandmother took some of the gloss off her fairytale evening, but Seb continued to dominate her thoughts. *Dream of me*, he had said. Asleep or awake, she knew her mind would be full of red-blooded images of the man who stirred her as no one else ever had.

A cough and an incoherent murmur drew her attention to the figure in the other bed. Hugging her pillow, Gina frowned, lying so she was facing her grandmother, ready to go to her should she need anything. Listening for breathing problems and further coughing, she closed her eyes, reliving every moment with Seb. She might be the biggest fool imaginable, but she could not wait for the night hours to pass—because when the morning came she would be seeing him again.

Seb strode through Elba's hospital in Portoferraio, a mix of emotions churning inside him. When he had arrived at the bed and breakfast that morning, eager to see Gina, to spend the day with her and her grandmother, he had been shocked to be greeted by an anxious Signora Mancini with the news that Maria had been taken ill during the night. Gina, he'd been told, had taken the older woman to hospital in a taxi at dawn.

His first concern had been for Maria's health. Then, on his drive to the island's main town, he had worried for Gina, knowing how upset and alarmed she must be. Even though she was a nurse, when something happened to someone you loved it was hard to hold on to the professional balance. But he also couldn't help the sting of hurt that Gina had not turned to him for help—had not thought to ring him so he could drive them to the hospital. OK, she had no idea about his medical knowledge, but given everything that had passed between them, albeit in less than twenty-four hours, he would have liked her to trust him, to want him with her.

Leaving her the night before had been the most difficult thing he had ever done. Back at the villa, unable to settle, thinking about her, wanting her, needing her, he had discovered a message on the answer-machine from Rico. His cousin had informed him he had the information he wanted from Scotland. He had phoned back right away.

'Everything checked out,' Rico had confirmed. 'Nic knows them—something to do with their dog and Gina's new job. He says they are one hundred per cent genuine in every way.'

It hadn't been a surprise—not after meeting Maria and spending the evening with Gina—but the relief after his experience with Antonella had been huge. 'Thank you.' In his heart he had known, and he had felt guilty for doubting her, disgusted with himself for being so cynical, especially when Gina herself was so open, so giving.

'How was your evening?' Rico had asked, and Seb hadn't been able to halt the smile that had spread across his face.

'Great.' He'd filled his cousin in on Maria's mission to scatter Matthew's ashes. 'I thought Zio Roberto and Zia Sofia would have no problem with me helping her.'

'Count on it. Do what you think is right, Seb. No one but us will know if there isn't an official permit—and it's our private beach. It's a really touching story.'

He'd been glad to have Rico's backing and understanding. 'It is.'

'So, what's she like?'

'Frail, not in *bad* health for seventy—although she has arthritis and a few niggling problems. Especially with her breathing. She didn't feel well enough to come to dinner.'

Rico had laughed. 'I meant the *granddaughter*—Gina!'

'Oh.' Seb hadn't been able to make sense of his reaction to Gina himself, let alone try to explain them to his cousin. 'She's…'

'…got to you,' Rico had finished for him when he'd hesitated. 'If she's a tall curvy blonde I'll come over to Elba and check her out for myself.'

'Well, she's not. So you can keep away.'

Seb had cursed the tell-tale snap in his voice, the defensiveness he had been unable to mask. As much as he loved his cousin, he didn't want Rico here, exuding his renowned charm, good-looks and sex appeal on Gina!

'Message received. But now I am even more curious,' Rico had teased. 'Gina must be something else if she has you, always so cool and uninvolved, all possessive and tied in knots after a couple of hours!'

'I'm not possessive—or tied in knots,' he had lied.

'Right!' His half-hearted protest hadn't fooled Rico. 'I can hear it in your voice *cugino*. And you had a cosy dinner for two! Tell me you told her the truth about your identity?'

'I'm not ready to say anything yet.'

'You mean you're worried how Gina will react if she finds out you have money and fame,' Rico had interjected, with alarming insight.

He hadn't known how to explain. 'Being with Gina today made me realise that I don't like what I've been the last few years. I'm not sure I'll ever come to terms with losing surgery, but I never should have moved so far from my roots.'

'It's clear she's made an impression on you.'

'I've only known her a few hours.'

'Sometimes these things happen that fast,' Rico had counselled. 'Just don't leave it too long to tell her, Seb. Not if you want to take things further with her. Or this is going to come back to bite you.'

There had been genuine worry in his cousin's voice, and Seb had experienced a few lingering doubts that he was doing the right thing. 'I'll think about it.' But he was scared that the truth would change Gina's view of him.

Now, at the hospital, as he found out where Maria had been taken and went in search of Gina, he knew he was walking a fine line. People here knew him, and it was a risk if he wanted to keep Gina from finding out. Of course he could tell her himself, but this was not the time or place— not while Gina was sidetracked and troubled about her grandmother's health. He *would* tell her…when they were both ready. For now he had to negotiate his way carefully through the minefield ahead, and his main focus was on how Gina was coping and on Maria's well-being.

Turning a corner, he spied Gina sitting alone in a stark corridor, wearing faded jeans and a short-sleeved, button-fronted red top. One trainer-clad foot was tapping in agitation and her hands were knotted together in her lap. A wave of tenderness overwhelmed him. She glanced up as he closed the gap between them, surprise in her anxious dark eyes, swiftly followed by a gratifying expression of welcome relief. With a tremulous smile, she rose to her feet and stepped into his waiting arms. Seb gathered her close, wanting to shield her, protect her, comfort her, grateful that she clung to him as if she trusted him and found solace with him.

He drew back a fraction to examine her face, finding her pale and strained. With the fingers of one hand he brushed away some stray strands of hair that had escaped her hurried ponytail.

'Are you all right?'

She nodded, still leaning against him. 'Yes. Thank you for coming.'

'You should have called me,' he chided softly, stroking her cheek.

'It happened so quickly.' She shook her head, worry reflected in her eyes. 'Nonna deteriorated suddenly, and rather than waiting for an ambulance or bothering you, Signora Mancini called the man who lives next door to her, who runs the taxi. I'm sorry.'

Seb cursed himself for letting his selfish feeling of rejection add to Gina's concern. 'You did the right thing. I just wish I had been there for you both. Tell me what happened,' he instructed, sitting her down, then taking the place beside her, keeping hold of her hand.

'You heard my grandmother coughing last night?' she began, and he nodded, recalling Maria's moments of discomfort and her disturbed breathing. 'That only started in the last couple of days. She assured me she was just tired after the journey from Scotland. When I got back last night—' a becoming flush warmed her cheeks, and Seb's own blood heated; he knew she was thinking of their passionate kisses '—she was asleep, but restless, her breathing irregular. She worsened near dawn and complained of chest pain, breathlessness, and the cough was more persistent.'

'And have they told you anything?' Feeling her shaking, he slipped an arm around her and drew her close.

'No. Nothing.' She gave a wry laugh. 'I know what hospitals are like, but it's different being on the other side.'

Seb knew that all too well after his experiences the last couple of months following his knife-wounds. 'I'll see what I can find out. I know it is easy to say, Gina, but try not to worry. Maria is in good hands here.'

Cupping her face, wishing he could do more to ease her

burden, he placed an all-too-brief kiss on her parted lips. He hated leaving her alone again, even for a few minutes, but hoped he could quietly use his influence here to get some details about Maria's condition and bring Gina some reassuring news.

Gina cursed herself for failing to alert Seb about what had happened and cancel their arrangement for the day. He had been on her mind, but she had been so overwhelmed by her anxiety for her grandmother that she had delayed calling him. Had she secretly hoped he would follow them to Portoferraio? She honestly wasn't sure. But when she had looked up and seen him walking towards her, casually dressed in jeans, black T-shirt, and a cream jumper that highlighted his dark good looks, the rush of pleasure at his presence, followed by the relief of being held in his arms, had been indescribable. She was grateful for his support, and his concern for her grandmother. Language was no barrier, but she was a stranger here, and having Seb on her side made her feel immeasurably better and no longer alone.

The wait seemed endless, and yet it could not have been long before Seb was striding back towards her, the smile on his face lifting a massive weight of worry from her shoulders. She rose to meet him, allowing him to take her hands, needing the contact, warmed by the comfort his touch brought.

'Did you discover anything?' she queried, eager for news.

'Maria is doing well. I have seen her, Gina, and I will take you to her now.' A welter of emotions assailed her—relief, gratitude, impatience to see her grandmother, and puzzlement that Seb, exuding a calm control over the situation, seemed to have gained such swift access to her grandmother. 'Maria has a chest infection. They are doing an X-ray, then tests to see if it is viral or bacterial and whether she will need antibiotics or not. In the meantime she is having fluids to rehydrate her, and paracetamol to lower her temperature.'

'There's nothing wrong with her heart?' she asked, voicing her secret fear.

Seb shook his head. 'Nothing at all. Her heart is strong. I promise.'

'I was so scared.' She bit her lip, trying to stop her voice from trembling. 'I couldn't bear to lose her, too.'

'I know, *tesoro*.'

She sank against him as he wrapped his arms around her once more. It felt so good to have someone else to lean on for once. For so long she had been the strong one, shouldering all the responsibility at home, coping with a stressful job, scared after Malcolm's treachery to allow any man into her life. She buried her face against Seb, breathing in his scent, absorbing his strength. It had all happened so quickly. While the initial attraction remained, and physically she wanted him, she already cared about him, felt an emotional bond she couldn't explain. She was moved by his innate goodness, affected as much by his tender touches as his fiery passion.

'Come, now,' he murmured, stroking her hair, making her feel safe and cared for. 'The doctor is waiting to talk with you.'

'Thank you.'

She fought back tears of relief, feeling bereft when he released her. Scrambling to gather up her bag, she wondered how she could have missed the signs that her grandmother had been brewing a worrying chest infection. She never should have let her make this journey. If only—

'Gina, stop.'

Seb's gentle admonishment interrupted her self-recriminations, and she glanced at him with a frown. 'Sorry?'

'You are blaming yourself,' he challenged with frightening insight. 'Don't, *cara*. It is not your fault.'

'But I'm a nurse. I care for her. I should have *seen*,' she protested.

'Maria didn't want you to see.' He cupped her face. 'This trip meant so much to her that she hid from you how she was feeling.'

Gina's eyes widened in shock. 'Nonna told you that?'

'Yes. She feels guilty now for any trouble and worry she has caused you.' Seb rested one hand at the small of her back as they walked along the corridor. 'Soon she will tell you so you know this for yourself.'

When they stepped into the small room, Gina's gaze flew straight to the figure propped up in the bed. Her grandmother looked frail, but much more comfortable than when she had last seen her. Oblivious to the doctor and nurse in the room, Gina hurried across to give the woman she loved so much a hug, careful of the drip in her arm. For a moment she experienced a strange mix of emotions…feeling both the responsibility of an adult and yet almost like a little girl again.

'I am sorry, *ragazza mia*. So sorry. But I knew you would make me stay at home, and I *had* to come to Elba to do this for my Matteo…whatever the consequences.' Gina saw regret mix with determination in the wise hazel eyes. 'Forgive me.'

'Oh, Nonna…Of course I forgive you. I just want you well,' she reassured her, trying to smile and hide how frightened she had been.

She sensed Seb moving up behind her, and instinctively she reached for his hand, grateful when he linked his fingers with hers, making her feel stronger.

'Gina, meet the doctor who is looking after Maria.' Seb drew her attention to the small grey-haired man who politely dismissed the nurse and then moved towards the bed. 'This is Dottore Franco Vasari.'

She shook hands, relieved that the kindly doctor immediately inspired confidence. Slipping easily back into Italian, she questioned him about her grandmother's health.

'As you can see, Signora McNaught looks much better than when she came to us this morning.' Dottore Vasari's smile encompassed them all. 'Soon we will have the results and know the nature of the infection, and then we will decide which medication to choose, and whether antibiotics are needed.' He seated himself on the edge of the bed. 'We will continue with intravenous rehydration for the time being. I would like to keep her in for twenty-four hours, for rest and observation.'

Although her grandmother looked disgusted at the idea, Gina nodded. 'Whatever you think is best. But we are only booked to stay on Elba for two more nights,' she explained, noting the doctor's frown and feeling the way Seb's fingers momentarily tightened on hers.

'I would not be happy for Signora McNaught to travel so soon,' Dottore Vasari insisted, glancing at the notes. 'Flying home in two days would not be sensible. I recommend you extend your stay for a little longer. I will write a letter for your own doctor that you can take home for follow-up care.' He rose to his feet and handed cards to herself and Seb. 'I will leave you now to talk things over. I shall be checking on your grandmother regularly, *signorina*, and hope to discharge her at midday tomorrow. If you have any questions or concerns, please call me.'

'Thank you. I'm very grateful,' Gina told him, shaking hands again.

She was confused at the older man's almost deferential nod towards Seb, but her grandmother was reclaiming her attention, and she had no more time to ponder on Seb's authoritative and knowledgeable manner.

'Gina, if I must stay in this place I will not have you sitting here fretting all day,' her grandmother insisted, recovering much of her spirit. 'You have dreamed all your life of seeing Elba. I will be cared for here. You must go and explore the island.'

'But—'

'No arguments, *ragazza mia*! Do it for me. Please? Besides, there will be arrangements to make if we must stay longer,' her grandmother pointed out.

Already Gina was making a mental list. She needed to find an internet café to contact the airline and change their tickets. Then she needed to check with the insurance company about health cover, plus e-mail home with the news. Thank goodness she had another week before starting her new job at the centre.

'I'll sort things out, Nonna,' she promised.

Her grandmother shook her head. 'You will have to find somewhere else for us to stay, Gina. Signora Mancini has already told me that our room is booked for other guests the day we were meant to leave. She has no more vacancies.'

'Don't worry.' Gina smothered a sigh, trying not to think of how depleted her small contingency fund might be at the end of this unexpected change of plan.

'*Scusi.*' Seb stepped forward, addressing them both. 'There is no question but you must come to stay at the villa for your extra days on the island.'

Gina's eyes widened. 'What about the owners? Won't they mind?' she protested, both relieved and concerned at the prospect of staying with Seb.

'The Linardi family will be pleased to help. Indeed, they will insist on it. There is no problem, Gina, I assure you,' he promised, wearing down her shaky resistance.

With funds low, it would be a great help not to have to move to a more expensive hotel. But she was determined to pay for their keep at the villa, whatever Seb decreed. It would be dangerously tempting to live in the same house as him, and it put wickedly improper thoughts in her mind. And in Seb's, if the sultry expression in his eyes was anything to go by. A shiver of sensual excitement rippled through her.

'That would be marvellous!' her grandmother exclaimed, more colour returning to her cheeks. 'I would be closer to the special place I shared with Matteo, no?'

Smiling, Seb took her grandmother's hand. 'Exactly. And when you are well, Maria, we can take care of the task you came here to accomplish.'

'Thank you.' Her grandmother's whispered words and

the longing on her face brought tears to Gina's eyes. 'You are both so good to me.'

'Then it is settled. Gina and I will see to the necessary arrangements and have things ready for you to come home tomorrow afternoon.'

'That sounds like so much work for you both,' her grandmother worried.

'Not at all.' Seb turned to Gina, a private promise in his eyes that fired her blood. 'It will not take long. Then I will show Gina the island. Whatever she wishes. And later we will come back to see you, Maria. How is that?'

Her grandmother all but clapped her hands in delighted acceptance. 'Perfect!'

The decision made, they said their goodbyes and left the older woman to rest. Gina's mind was buzzing—not only with the tasks ahead of her, but with delight at spending time alone with Seb and nervousness at staying at the villa. She didn't know how she would resist temptation. Should she even try?

Seb took her hand, his fingers linking with hers, his touch spiking her pulse. Once outside in the sunshine, he turned her to face him, his hands resting on her shoulders as she leaned against the car.

'Gina, I need you to understand something.'

Her heart beating crazily beneath her ribs, she gazed into molten caramel-coloured eyes. 'What is it?'

'The invitation to stay at the villa comes without strings,' he told her, his hands moving until his palms cupped her face. 'There is no pressure, Gina. No obligation or expectation. I will help you and Maria, whatever happens between us.' He paused a moment, his eyes darkening as his gaze dropped to her mouth, his voice turning huskier. 'Yes, I want you. I want you as I have never wanted anyone before. But only if it is what you want, too. It is your choice…if and when you are ready.'

His honesty, reassurance and understanding made her

respect and care about him even more. Electricity hummed between them. She felt strong, centred, yet giddy with excitement, alive with desire, feeling her true power as a woman in a way she never had before. Seb was changing her. She was growing in confidence because of him. She wanted him…badly. No matter what the future held for them, she knew she would forever regret not taking this chance with Seb. She might live the rest of her life and never experience anything this amazing again. The time she had with him might be short, but there was nothing casual about the way she felt for him.

Reaching up, she kissed him. The passion was there, but so was something much deeper—an emotional connection that took them to a whole new level. Pulling back, she rested a palm against his jaw.

'Thank you.'

Seb nodded, seeming to understand without the need for words. 'Let's go and take care of business, then we can enjoy our day together and see where it takes us.'

CHAPTER FIVE

'I COULDN'T eat another thing,' Gina protested, rejecting Seb's offer of more fruit and flopping back on the grass with a sigh. 'That was the best picnic I've ever had.'

Chuckling to himself, Seb packed away the remains of the food he had bought in Portoferraio, while Gina had been at the internet café changing travel arrangements, dealing with the insurance and checking her e-mails. Afterwards, they had briefly explored some of the interesting places in Elba's capital town before he had brought her to this quiet beauty spot for their lunch.

Enjoying being close, he lay on his back beside her and reached for her hand, curling their fingers together. 'What do you do to relax at home?'

'I read. And I love walking, swimming and cycling. My friends and I go ten-pin bowling or to the cinema. Sometimes we stay in with pizza and wine and just chat.'

'But no dating?' he murmured, turning on his side and propping himself on one elbow so he could study her.

'No dating.'

Her eyes were closed, long lashes fanning her cheeks, and the dappled sunlight filtered through the trees, kissing her face. 'What happened? With the man you were seeing four years ago?' he added, as her lashes lifted and he found himself looking into solemn dark eyes.

'Malcolm was in hospital management. He was charming, persistent…I was flattered. We'd been together nearly a year, and I thought things might go somewhere between us,' she admitted, and he felt a strange tightening inside him.

'You were in love with him?'

Gina looked thoughtful, but shook her head. 'I cared about him, and before all this happened I thought I could come to love him. But afterwards I was more hurt and angry at what he did than heartbroken that we had broken up. I could never have stayed with or loved someone like that—not when he showed his true colours. In the end, he wasn't the person I thought he was.'

'I see.'

Seb hesitated, feeling guilty because he hadn't told Gina the full truth about himself. What would she think of him when she discovered that? As he wrestled with his conscience—liking her, wanting her to like him, needing to be with her, but scared that if he told her it would drive her away—she continued with her story.

'My grandparents were becoming increasingly frail, and their Glasgow house was unsuitable, so I persuaded them to move in with me. Malcolm didn't like it. He turned surly, rude and demanding—to them as well as to me.' She shifted restlessly and he brushed his thumb across her wrist as her fingers tightened on his. 'Then he issued an ultimatum. He'd gone behind my back and made enquiries about residential homes. He called my grandparents horrible names, referred to Nonna as "the old crone", and said I either put them in the place he had found or he walked.'

'*Bastardo,*' Seb swore, hating the man for hurting Gina and disrespecting her grandparents, for his selfishness and lack of understanding.

A ghost of a smile curved her mouth. 'I said something similar. There was no choice at all—not for me. My grandparents meant everything to me, and no way was Malcolm, or anyone else, coming between us.'

'He had no idea of the importance of family.' Leaning down, his lips whispered softly over hers. 'I'm sorry, Gina.'

'It was a long time ago—we weren't meant to be. Things were unpleasant at the hospital for a while. Malcolm made remarks about me. But support was on my side and thankfully he got a job elsewhere soon afterwards and moved away.'

No wonder she had been wary of getting involved again, and had put that part of her life on hold, unsure who she could trust, concerned that whoever she dated wouldn't under-stand her loyalties and responsibilities. As far as he was con-cerned they only made her more attractive, more special.

Gina sat up beside him, wrapping her arms around her knees, affording him a tantalising glimpse of the small dolphin tattoo at the base of her spine. Unable to help himself, he reached out and traced the shape of the leaping form with his fingertips, feeling her response to his touch in the ripple of her skin.

'This is pretty,' he murmured.

'Thank you.' A mischievous smile curved her mouth as she looked down at him, and he didn't know what he wanted most—to taste her kiss or set his lips to her tattoo. 'I had it done when I was eighteen.'

'Why a dolphin?'

A reminiscent look crossed her face and her smile faded. 'I think I heard nearly as many stories about my grandfa-ther's time at sea as I did about Elba when I was growing up. He often saw dolphins—they were his good luck symbol—joy and spirit and freedom. He took me to see them off the Scottish coast once. It was amazing. I'm a Pisces…I love the water. I love dolphins and I love my grandfather. Instead of the fish of my star sign, I chose this.'

'I like it.' It was symbolic of her—her loyalties, her loves. His fingers lingered a moment more, then he moved, sitting up before he gave in to temptation and drew her down to the grass again, to spend the next few hours kissing her all over. 'We have the afternoon ahead of us. If you could do anything you wanted, go anywhere on the island, what would you choose?'

'I want to see *everything*,' she confessed with a laugh. 'I've been in love with the idea of Elba all my life, and have read everything I can find about it—from the many invasions over the centuries to Napoleon Bonaparte's exile here in 1814.'

His insides knotted when she smiled at him, her dark eyes sparkling with interest and delight.

'I want to see Napoleon's country villa at San Martino, the island's mineralogical museums and old mines, the Medieval and Renaissance fortresses, the Roman villas, the hidden churches and shrines, and to explore the unspoilt landscape.'

'I don't think we'll squeeze all those in before returning to see Maria this evening,' he teased, enchanted by Gina, her freshness and natural beauty.

'Spoilsport,' she accused with a mock pout, which focused his attention back on her delicious mouth.

He clenched his hands to fists to stop himself reaching for her and forgetting all about sightseeing. 'Pick one,' he requested, hearing the roughness of desire in his voice.

'Marciana Alta.'

The oldest settlement on Elba, with origins dating back to 35BC, the medieval village was perched on the mountainside. Seb was unsurprised by her choice. Rising to his feet, he took her hand and drew her up, unable to resist one more kiss, lingering as she moaned, her response eager and immediate. He had meant everything he had said to her earlier. Anything further that happened between them would be Gina's choice. But he couldn't help grasping these stolen moments when they came his way. Before things got out of hand, he set her away from him. Her cheeks were flushed, her lips rosy and plump. Smothering a groan, he dredged up every atom of control he could muster and led the way back to the car.

Before long, they had reached the picturesque village. Gina's enthusiasm was infectious, and sharing this with her was like seeing it all again through fresh eyes. They visited the archaeological museum, with its Paleolithic, Etruscan and Roman finds, walked the narrow alleyways and cobbled lanes of red-tiled houses, their doorways festooned with colourful flowers, and saw the crumbling remains of the Pisan fortress.

'Are you scared of heights?' he asked a while later.

'No. Why?'

'Would you like to take the cableway to the summit of Monte Capanne? It's the highest mountain on the island at over one thousand metres. On a clear day you can see as far as Corsica from the top.'

She looked almost childlike in her delight, her eyes wide, her smile broad. 'I'd love that. Can we go?'

'Of course,' he agreed, happy to indulge her.

He had never spent time with a woman like this, and he was amazed at how much he was loving it. His desire for Gina was ever-present, but the longer he was with her the more relaxed he felt, the more he liked her, and the more he came to realise how false the life he had been living—and the people in it—had become. He could also now admit how much he hated it…and himself for ever getting caught up in it in the first place. The reconstructive surgery he'd used to do full-time might not have paid so well, but it had been more emotionally and professionally rewarding.

Seb had decisions to make about his future. The loss of money didn't bother him, nor did he care about the ending of a fame he had never wanted, nor the loss of the hangers-on, the so-called glamour, the women who had used him for their own ends. What he *did* care about was the loss of his ability to perform surgery. The enlightenment that he had taken a wrong turning had come too late—he had been too caught up in the moment to recognise it. Having to take a step back due to his injuries, combined with meeting

Gina, was opening his eyes, making him reassess his life and his priorities.

'Are you all right?'

Gina's soft query drew him from his dark thoughts. He saw the confused frown on her face and the concern in her eyes. What would she think of him if she knew? He couldn't tell her. Not yet. He didn't want to spoil this special time with her.

'I'm fine,' he reassured her with a smile, pushing his self-doubt to the back of his mind. 'Let's take that ride up the mountain.'

The base of the cableway was only a short distance from the village, and they were soon climbing into one of the yellow open-framed metal cradles which held only a couple of people. Gina stepped in first and Seb followed.

'This is cosy!' She glanced over her shoulder and smiled at him.

'Mmm.' Standing behind her, he wrapped his arms around her waist, relishing the feel of her snuggling back against him. 'Perfect for two.'

They journeyed upwards, suspended precariously over crags and crevices, chestnut and holm oak woods, ancient vineyards and a wide array of native fauna and flora. Encouraged by Gina's interest, he pointed out places they could spot across the island.

'The view is amazing,' she exclaimed, her gaze focused on the rugged coast and across the sea far below to other islands in the chain.

'It is,' he agreed softly, captivated by the graceful curve of her neck, her profile, the expression of wonderment on her face.

Dipping his head, he nudged the satin fall of her hair aside and nuzzled against her neck, hearing her soft moan as his lips worked their way to the sensitive hollow beneath her ear, his tongue-tip tasting her skin. She smelled of vanilla, sunshine and Gina. He didn't think he'd ever get enough of her. As she leaned back into him, he flattened his palms on the rounded curve of her belly, nibbling her ear as he inched up towards the tempting jut of her breasts.

Glancing down, he could see her nipples had beaded to tight peaks. Her breathing turned ragged and she gasped when he finally skimmed the rest of the way up her body and cupped her fullness, shaping gently, grazing across her taut nipples. Her hands tightened their grip on the cradle railing. Arching to his touch, she dropped her head back, and his mouth took advantage of more exposed skin, gently biting at her, salving with strokes of his tongue. He wanted more. Wanted to see her, taste her.

Then a noise from above reminded him where they were and he groaned, sliding his hands back down to her waist, holding her steady as they both fought for control in the few moments before they reached the mountain top and exited the cradle. For a while they lingered to enjoy the view, arms around each other, then rode the cableway back down to the village.

'It's time to head back to the hospital,' he told her as they returned to the car. 'Will you come to the villa for a meal afterwards?'

'Thank you. But I'll have to go back to Signora Mancini's tonight.'

Her words dampened his hopes. 'Are you sure? You're welcome to stay.'

'I know.'

'I don't like to think of you being there alone,' he commented, knowing that was partly true, but equally that he just didn't want to let her go.

She met his gaze, a small smile playing at her mouth. 'I'll be fine. There are things I need to do before tomorrow.'

'OK.'

He tried to be satisfied with that, to tamp down his disappointment. He had promised not to rush her, and he wouldn't, but that didn't mean he wouldn't miss her.

All he could hope was that Gina would come to want
him as much as he wanted her.

Gina wriggled onto a high stool at the counter in the villa's
impressive kitchen, watching Seb move around with casual
ease, gathering things together to make them a quick meal
before taking her back to Signora Mancini's. Having
promised the woman by phone that she would return with
news and stay a final night, Gina felt obligated to keep her
word. She also needed to do the packing for herself and her
grandmother. But she had sensed that Seb's unspoken reluctance matched her own. She didn't want to leave him,
but the timing and the circumstances weren't right. Not
until her grandmother was safely out of hospital and settled
in the guest suite Seb had shown her on a quick tour of the
large, single-storey villa.

'Maria was looking better, *tesoro*, no?'

'Much better. It's a big relief to know there is apparently
nothing more serious going on than a mild flu-like virus
and some pleural inflammation,' she continued, feeling a
big weight of worry had been lifted off her shoulders.

Her grandmother had been in much better spirits, her
breathing easier, and with more colour in her cheeks after
a restful day. The X-ray had revealed a small amount of
fluid on the lungs, but tests had shown the cause was not
bacterial so no antibiotics would be needed. Instead she had
been prescribed diuretic tablets to help clear the lungs and
prevent any increase in the oedema which was starting to
show in puffy ankles, the skin pitting when pressed and
slow to return to normal. She had also been given some
anti-inflammatories to ease the pleural discomfort that had
caused the chest pain and made breathing painful lying
down in the night.

'We'll get things checked out with our own GP when
we get home.'

Nodding, Seb stroked one hand over her hair as he

passed her. 'A good idea to follow things up,' he agreed. A small frown creased her brow as she recalled how unfazed he had been at the hospital on their second visit at the end of the day, how interested in and understanding of what was happening to her grandmother.

Gina bit her lip as she thought over the various possibilities that could lie behind her grandmother's symptoms. 'Dottore Vasari suggested it might be poor circulation that's causing the water retention and leading to fluid on the lungs.'

'A few days rest here, where we shall watch over her and pamper her, and Maria should be much improved,' Seb promised with a smile.

And then they would be able to return home. Gina didn't want to think of that part, much as she wanted her grandmother well again. Smothering a sigh, she folded her arms and leaned on the counter, watching Seb work, already enjoying the aromas that were starting to emerge from the dish he was preparing for them. He seemed so proficient, and it made her realise how little she really knew about him—how seldom she could encourage him to talk about himself.

'Have you always liked cooking?'

'It's something I've come to enjoy more and more in recent years,' he confided, starting to chop fresh tomatoes and local, seasonal porcini mushrooms.

Gina noted the intermittent trouble he had with the function of his right hand, his chopping action awkward. She wanted to ask him more about his injury, wanted to offer to help with the chores, but she refrained from commenting, knowing that he wouldn't talk about it and would resent her fussing. The grimace on his face as he wielded the knife attested to his own annoyance and impatience with his limitations. So she remained silent, allowing him to concentrate on his task while her own thoughts turned to the events of the day.

She had no idea how they had crammed so much into a

few hours. But they had covered a great deal of ground, and she was exhausted but happy—especially since finding her grandmother in such good form. Sightseeing with Seb had been a wonderful experience. He had been a patient and knowledgeable companion, and being with him had made the day so much more special—particularly given all the kissing and hand-holding and touching. A flush warmed her cheeks as she remembered those stolen moments on the cableway, and how incredible it had felt to have him caress her.

What had begun as basic attraction and physical desire had turned into so much more. The more time she spent with Seb, the more she cared about him. He was warm and funny, intelligent, and unfailingly kind. He mixed exquisite gentleness with intense passion. She felt comfortable with him—could talk to him, share with him as deeply, if not more, as she did with her close friends. She could explain her feelings and concerns in a way she couldn't with her grandmother for fear of worrying her. Seb made her feel like a real woman again, desired and feminine, and being romanced by such a stunning and sexy man was incredibly exciting. That he was so understanding and good to her grandmother made him more irresistible.

Seb slid a plate in front of her, adding cutlery and a glass of chilled spring water, his warm smile sparking a new tingle of awareness inside her.

'Thank you for this,' she said as he served her a generous portion of pasta and an aromatic sauce topped with freshly grated Parmesan cheese. 'Mmm—it looks wonderful.'

'Tell me more about your new job,' he requested as he sat opposite her.

'With all the new investment in our area, the local council and health authority are taking advantage of private and charitable donations and opening a new drop-in centre,' she began, pausing to take a sip of her water. 'The plan is to provide a wide range of health and social care, bringing services, advice, support and information together under one roof for those who have difficulty coping or accessing mainline health facilities.'

With an impatient sigh, Seb switched his fork from his uncooperative right hand to his left and resumed attempts to twirl his spaghetti around it. 'Who has difficulty getting health care from the hospital or local doctors, and why?'

'You'd be surprised how many people can't or won't use the services provided—and for a whole variety of reasons: fear, suspicion, lack of knowledge. The centre is designed to help the homeless, migrants and refugees, people with drink and drug addictions, those with HIV/AIDS.'

'What does the centre offer?' Seb queried.

Encouraged by his interest, her enthusiasm for what they were trying to do in Strathlochan bubbled through. 'We have clinics for minor injuries, wound care and dressing changes, vaccinations, TB screening, contraception and sexually transmitted diseases. We offer clean needles, also drugs, alcohol and AIDS awareness, and dentistry for those having difficulty accessing NHS dental care. Counselling, chiropody—all kinds of health and social advice… Whatever problems are presented by those who come to us we try to tackle—medical and social. There is a small hostel attached with washing facilities and short-term beds. And we also have a mentoring scheme, where one-on-one help is offered to those making an effort to get off the streets, off drugs, off alcohol and into work and a safe place to live.'

'It sounds excellent,' Seb praised, genuine admiration in his voice.

'I think it's a worthwhile project,' she admitted, looking up to find him studying her intently. 'I want to feel I am helping to make a difference, even in a small way.'

'You are doing a good thing—an important thing.'

'Thank you.'

She followed his lead and continued with her meal, puzzled by the unidentified edge that had been in his voice, the look of sadness and regret that had briefly crossed his expression before he had masked it.

'What about staffing?' he asked after a moment.

'The regular team consists of Dr Thornton Gallagher, who is the clinical director in charge of the centre, a specialist psychologist, a counsellor, and two other nurses besides myself,' she told him, savouring the last bites of the delicious meal. 'For the time being we don't have the funds to employ full-time doctors or a dentist on staff, so we rely on the goodwill of numerous doctors and other local healthcare professionals from the hospital and surrounding GP and dental practices. Everyone has joined forces to back the project, and they volunteer their time to run our clinics. If the centre is a success, we hope funds will be available to expand the full-time medical team.'

Listening to Gina speak with such passion about her work gave Seb even more to think about in terms of his own situation. When had he last felt that real fire in his belly, or had the satisfaction of knowing he was helping people who really needed him? In recent years that genuine fulfilment had only come with his *pro bono* patients. As much as he loved surgery, he had lost his enjoyment and gained little professional or personal gratification from vanity work. Gina, with her honesty and dedication, stripped it all down to the basics, to the things that really mattered most. Need and care. It made him ashamed of the way he had wasted his talents. Perhaps he had deserved to lose them.

His physical scars were fading, and daily exercise was helping his injuries to heal, although he still experienced reduced function plus some numbness and discomfort. He probably always would. But the mental scars at losing his surgical career were harder to come to terms with. What was he going to do with the rest of his life? Was he going to stay in medicine? If not, what else *could* he do? These were the questions he had escaped Florence to answer. Alone on Elba, away from press intrusion, and the understandable but smothering concern of Zio Roberto and Zia Sofia, he had sought privacy to face his future and make decisions.

Maybe things were not as hopeless as he had feared. True, he couldn't operate again, and the knowledge still grieved him. He'd worked so hard and for so long to prove himself that it felt like failure to give in. But meeting Gina, hearing her speak with such passion about her work, posed new questions, and made him look at things in a different way. There were other areas of medicine open to him— other things he could do to make a difference. He could still help people, still heal them. Rico would give him a post at his clinic any time he asked, but that line of work was not for him. What he had to do was find a new niche for himself...and Gina was helping point him in a new and more promising direction.

'How do you feel about people who live on the street?' he found himself asking, playing devil's advocate, shocking himself that he was stepping out on a limb, touching on something he never discussed. 'Many would say that those with the kinds of problems you've mentioned are beyond help, or are taking funds away from others.'

'Well, they'd be wrong. People end up in those circumstances for all kinds of reasons, and they deserve our care and attention the same as anyone else,' Gina riposted, her dark eyes full of sincerity and fire as she met his gaze. Pushing aside her empty plate, she leaned her forearms on the counter. 'It can really narrow your world—make you feel you have nowhere to turn, no choices, no one who is interested in you. We're all one bad break away from needing help and understanding, and everyone is entitled to the care we can offer them.'

'That's true.' He hesitated, wondering whether to take this further, and then Gina herself continued, surprising him anew.

'Both my father and grandfather were made redundant from the shipyards during a time of recession. The industry was being run down. Life was hard. We lost our home, and Mum, Dad and I had to go and live with Nonno Matthew and Nonna Maria. No one had any money. I was ten, but I remember the worry, the adults' constant search for work, the struggle for food, clothes and basics, the feeling of exclusion.'

Seb's heart turned over as she drew in a shaky breath and ducked her head. He took one hand in his, linking their fingers, moved by her story. How stupid of him that he had never once asked about her parents. He had been so focused on Maria—sidetracked by Gina's devoted care of her grandparents—that he had never thought to look more deeply into her motivations, her childhood, her mother and father.

'Gina…'

'Word came of possible jobs on Tyneside, in the yards there. My parents went there but things didn't work out. They were returning to Glasgow when they were killed in a train crash.'

'I am sorry, *tesoro*.'

She shook her head, her voice soft and sad, and his gut tightened. 'It was a long time ago.'

'So your grandparents raised you from the age of ten?'

'Yes. They took me in, cared for me, loved me, were always there for me,' she explained, a sheen of moisture shimmering in her eyes.

No wonder she felt so close to them, needed so badly to feel she was giving back. 'You're amazing.'

'No, I'm not. I told you because it shows that things can happen to anyone—we have no right to judge, to condemn. We don't know what it is like to walk in another person's shoes.'

'I spent a few years living on the streets.'

Seb didn't know why he was telling her. He certainly didn't want pity. Maybe he was testing her convictions, seeing how she would react—if she treated him differently, knowing of his past. He was used to people latching onto him because of who he was now—people who would despise him if they knew what his life had been like back then. Thankfully the reporters who had dug into his background had never discovered the full circumstances of his upbringing. Zio Roberto and Zia Sofia had surrounded him with their protection as well as their love.

He felt Gina's fingers tighten on his and he looked into her eyes. There was concern, understanding, sorrow…but no pity.

'What happened, Seb?'

Affected by the genuine interest in her softly voiced question, he found himself responding, telling her about his mother and those crazy years—things he had never told another living soul. Except Rico. But even his cousin didn't know all of it.

'My father died when I was young—an aortic aneurysm. Knowing his family disapproved of her and their marriage, thinking they would take me from her, my mother ran away with me the same night.' He paused a moment, closing his eyes as he recalled that confused flight from all that had been familiar. Swallowing, unable to look at Gina, he pressed on. 'My mother was unbalanced. Paranoid. Depressed. She drank too much. Took drugs. We lived hand to mouth and she dragged me around after her, moving from place to place…selling herself to buy us food and her next fix.'

'Oh, Seb.'

Gina's words were a mere whisper, but he nearly choked up at the depth of feeling they contained. He didn't stop her when she slid off her stool. Instead, he turned on his as she came around the counter and stepped up to him, hugging him tight. Burying his face in her hair, he breathed in her intoxicating scent, lingering a moment to absorb the comfort.

'Where did you go? How did you live?' she asked after a few moments.

'She'd shack up with a man for a while—usually someone who was dealing drugs and could get her what she needed. Mostly they tolerated having me around—sometimes not. Now and again we'd stay longer in one place, then things would go wrong and we'd move on again. One day, about three years after we had left home…' He hesitated as the events of that morning came back to him, as crystal-clear as if it had happened yesterday and not twenty-two years ago. 'She had one drink too many—one drug too many. I woke up and found her dead on the floor of the abandoned house we were squatting in.'

Gina's arms tightened around him, her cheek pressed to his so he felt the dampness of her tears. 'Oh, God. How old were you? What did you do?'

'I was eleven. And I was scared, alone. I didn't know anyone—didn't know where I was or what to do. So I ran. I knew how to survive on the streets, how to take care of myself, where to find restaurants who'd let me do some dirty jobs in return for leftover food or an outhouse to stay in overnight. I knew which market stalls wouldn't miss a few pieces of fruit, which bakeries threw out bread, where to go to scavenge discarded pizzas to fill my stomach.'

'No one helped you?'

He shook his head, touched that she sounded so scandalised on his behalf—like a fierce lioness about to go into battle to protect her cub. 'I didn't want help…I didn't trust anyone. But, unlike many street kids, I kept away from gangs and drugs. I spent hours in libraries devouring books, sneaking around museums, using their rest rooms, keeping warm and dry on bad days, using my brain.'

'And in the end?' Gina drew back a few inches, and he saw the residue of her tears spiking long sooty lashes. The fingers of one hand stroked along his jaw, firing his blood. 'How did you get out of that?'

'I got sick. Food poisoning. A priest found me on the street, barely conscious, and took me to a clinic run by the nuns. All I could tell them was my name.' Shaking his head, he took both Gina's hands in his and pressed a kiss to each palm in turn, feeling a quiver run through her. 'Unknown to me, my father's sister and her husband had never given up searching for me, and they had circulated my name and photograph. A nun recognised me and called them. Zio Roberto and Zia Sofia came to fetch me, and took me to their home to live with them and their son, Riccardo, who was my age. I was wild, scared, aloof, but they didn't give up,' he told her with a smile, recalling the endless patience, firmness and love that had finally turned him around.

Ever since then he had wanted to repay their generosity and acceptance by making something of himself, making them proud. Rico, the cousin who had befriended the suspicious, unruly boy, had been his rock, his confidant, his best friend, helping him catch up with school work. They had done everything together, including going to medical school. He'd felt driven to succeed—to prove to his aunt and uncle, and to Rico, that they had been right to invest their time in him. And to prove to himself that he was strong, that he could survive, could *be* something, that he was worthy of having people care about him. He hadn't realised quite how deeply his past still affected him until just now, telling Gina things he had never shared with anyone, including Rico.

'So there you have it—the grisly details of my life,' he said, trying to pass off the acute feeling of vulnerability he was experiencing with a false bravado.

'Don't make light of it,' Gina chided gently, curling her fingers with his, warmth and understanding in her expression. 'It can't have been easy to tell me, but I'm honoured that you did. Thank you. Your past is part of you, it's helped shape you, and you should be proud of yourself— of all that you have achieved.'

If confiding in Gina *had* unconsciously been a test, then she had passed with flying colours…and she had turned the tables on him. He felt uncharacteristically emotional. Needing a few moments to regain his equilibrium, he let go of her hands and rose to his feet, his voice husky and unsteady as he turned away from her and reached for their empty plates.

'You go out on the terrace and enjoy the view,' he suggested, praying she wouldn't argue. 'I'll clear up these things, then we can go to Signora Mancini's.'

She hesitated for an endless moment, and he held his breath, waiting. Then her hand briefly rubbed his back before it was withdrawn.

'OK.' He closed his eyes at the soft understanding and edgy emotion she didn't try to hide. 'Thanks for the meal, it was delicious.'

When Gina had left the kitchen, Seb poured himself a glass of water and drank it down. He'd thought he needed time alone, but already he missed her. And he sure as hell wished he had never agreed for her to spend the night at the bed and breakfast. He needed her here.

What was happening to him? He'd never experienced this kind of immediate rapport with anyone. Yes, he desired her. But it was so much more than just the physical, as important and urgent as that was. Gina accepted him. To her he was just Seb. His past didn't colour her view of him— she simply saw the person he was now, saw all that had gone before as making the whole. Yet he was horribly aware that he still hadn't told Gina the entire truth. He had held back because he was scared that when she knew what he had done with his career these last years she would see him differently, think less of him, judge him harshly—as he did himself. And he feared, too, that the reality of his fame and his money would irrevocably change things between them.

Confused, troubled, yet needing to be close to Gina every moment he could, he finished up and walked out to the terrace.

* * *

Gina leaned on the balustrade wall at the edge of the villa's expansive terrace, her mind buzzing with thoughts of all Seb had revealed to her about his past. Dusk was fading to the darkness of night, and moonlight played over the softly undulating surface of the sea beyond the cliffs. Neptune's Spear was a brooding shape, silhouetted offshore from the crescent of beach far below.

She ached for what Seb had borne as a young boy, ripped away from all that was safe following the death of his father, scared and confused by the erratic behaviour of a troubled mother on drink and drugs who'd flitted from man to man. And then to find her dead, to be left alone so young, trying to survive on the street... Thank God for the aunt and uncle who had searched for him and taken him in, given him a loving home and a secure future.

A proud and private man, it must have cost Seb to confide in her. And he'd been affected by the telling, she knew. She sensed he'd needed time alone to gather his thoughts...just as she'd had to stem her tears for the boy he had been. It seemed so unfair, given all he had been through in his youth, that he now faced what could be life-changing injuries to his hands—all due to a selfless act, helping someone in trouble. How worried he must be about being able to paint again. She wished she knew more about the damage to his nerves and tendons, the possible long-term effects, wished he wasn't so unwilling to talk about it or allow her to help him. There was so much she didn't know about him and his life...including how he had come to be on Elba, painting and acting as caretaker for this villa.

Gina felt rather than heard Seb approach behind her. A shiver of awareness rippled down her spine as he stepped up close and personal, his hands coming to rest either side of hers on top of the wall, his body brushing against her, trapping her in place. Flames of desire uncoiled inside her as the warmth of his breath fanned her skin. Soft, stolen kisses were followed by the teasing lick of his tongue, and when his teeth grazed against her, indulging in a gentle bite of possession, she whimpered, close to melting on the spot.

Succumbing to the urge, she turned in his arms, intending to... Well, she wasn't sure what she intended because the sultry intensity in his eyes banished every single thought from her brain. Seb raised a hand, his fingers whispering across her cheek before they glided along her neck, cupping her nape, holding her in place. She barely had time to draw in a shaky, fractured breath before his lips met hers in a bone-weakening, passionate kiss that instantly flared out of control. Her response was instinctive, inevitable, swamping her under a tidal wave of desire. His free arm wound round her waist, drawing her tight against him, while her own rose to link around his neck. He groaned, changing the angle, deepening the kiss, taking more, giving more, his tongue exploring, twining with hers, drawing her back into his own mouth, sucking on her. Gina lost herself in Seb, in heady passion, the ache of need deep inside her increasing and craving satisfaction.

They broke apart, just far enough and for long enough to drag oxygen into parched lungs, their panting breaths mingling, heartbeats thudding in a frantic dual rhythm. His voice was little more than a rough murmur when he spoke. 'I know this is fast.'

'It's crazy,' she murmured back.

'This thing between us is incredible.'

Gina couldn't deny it. 'Yes.'

'It is not a line, *tesoro*.' He switched to Italian, as if needing his first language to express the depth of his emotion. 'I have *never* felt like this about any woman before. I cannot explain it, to you or to myself, but from the first moment I saw you I was lost. There was an inner recognition, a meeting of souls.'

It was heady stuff, and she was unable to resist him or her own yearning. 'Seb.'

'Kissing you is wonderful. You're honey-sweet...' He

punctuated his praise with tormentingly brief caresses, nibbling her lips, teasing the corner of her mouth with his tongue-tip until she was frantic for more. 'But it's not enough, Gina. I need to see you, to touch you, to taste you everywhere, to fill you completely.'

'Oh, God.' The words trembled out of her as her mind filled with erotic images.

He lifted her so she was sitting on the terrace wall, his fingers skimming her jean-clad thighs, which parted of their own volition so he could step between them. She moaned, unable to stop herself wriggling closer, rubbing against the hard evidence of his arousal, desperate to ease the pressure that built within her. He continued to tease her with half-kisses and devastating strokes of his tongue, until she was forced to bury her hands in the thickness of his hair and take what she so urgently needed. He met and matched her hunger, his kiss pure sin. She couldn't get enough of him.

Seb was busy with the buttons of her top, and she quivered involuntarily at the exquisite touch of his fingers on her bare flesh. The pads of his thumbs were stroking circles around her navel, making her muscles tauten, and then his fingers skimmed her ribs, before his hands moved on to explore and caress her back. Lost in a slow, deep kiss, she was vaguely aware of him unsnapping the fastening of her bra, but it was only when he brushed the lacy cups aside and the fullness of her breasts spilled into his waiting palms that she gasped, her head dropping back, her hands leaving his hair to clasp his shoulders for support. He continued to torment her, tracing the outline of each breast, circling inwards, but never quite touching where she most needed him.

'Please,' she begged, unable to wait another second.

Seductive, heavy-lidded eyes watched her as she arched to his touch. Then his hands cupped her fully, firm and sure, and she cried out at the terrible joy of it, awash with sensation after sensation as he shaped her, caressed her, driving her crazy with want. Taut, sensitised nipples demanded attention, and darts of fire speared through her as his thumbs brushed over and around them. When she felt the cool evening breeze against her flaming skin, she opened her eyes, finding him watching her.

He waited endless moments, ignoring her pleas, feasting his gaze on her, then he lowered his head, and finally his mouth was there, warm and moist, teasing and tormenting her swollen nipple with lips, teeth and tongue. Just when she thought she couldn't bear it any longer, he closed his mouth around her and suckled her strongly inside, nearly sending her into orbit at the searing pleasure.

'Oh, Seb!'

It was too much…not enough. She writhed against him, seeking relief for the waves of ecstasy crashing over her. Her hands dragged at his jumper and the T-shirt beneath, needing to feel his skin. The fire threatened to consume them both. His own hands cupped her rear, pulling her tighter, and she locked her legs around his hips, pressing herself against him, wishing for all the world that two pairs of jeans were not separating them. Her flesh burned, her body craved fulfilment.

Slowly, noisily, reluctantly, his mouth released its prize, a rough moan escaping him as she dragged her fingernails along his spine.

'Gina, you are so beautiful, so responsive,' he murmured against her skin, working his way to her neglected breast at such a lingering pace she wanted to scream with frustration. 'Feel what you do to me,' he demanded, rocking more insistently against her, making her sob with the force of her desire. 'Making love is going to be indescribable for us.'

She had never felt so wanted. Had never been so out of control. Had never needed anyone with such desperate urgency. His mouth claimed her nipple, conducting the same sensual torture as it had to its twin, and she closed her eyes, arching to him, feeling the heat radiating off his skin, his muscles flexing under her fingers, the earthy, masculine fragrance of him making her light-headed.

'Stay with me. Please, Gina.'

'I can't. Not tonight,' she whispered, tempted almost beyond endurance. 'I have to go, Seb. We agreed.'

Seb cursed under his breath, trying to get his raging body back under some semblance of control. He could seduce Gina into his bed in an instant. They both knew it. Both wanted it with a desperation that was painful. But, foolishly, he had promised, so he had no one to blame but himself. With her grandmother on her mind, Gina was understandably distracted. If and when she came to him, he wanted it to be completely, knowingly, willingly, with nothing else to think about but the special magic between them.

Smothering a groan, he wrapped his arms around her and held her close, giving them both time to bank down the flames of passion that burned so fiercely between them. When he felt strong enough to behave, he drew back and reluctantly fixed her clothes back into place. It was a crime to cover up such voluptuous beauty, but he wanted no one seeing her or touching her but him. His task completed, he cupped her face in his hands, seeing the regret and the remaining sparks of desire in her soul-deep eyes.

'I'll drive you back.' He managed to force the words out, stepping away and helping her down off the wall, steadying her as she swayed. A draught of breeze rippled across the terrace, and he felt a shiver run through her as the heat of their passion subsided. 'You are cold, *tesoro.*'

Without waiting for her confirmation, he peeled off his jumper and helped her put it on, his body responding instinctively to the way she wrapped herself in it, closing her eyes and burying her face in the fabric, as if breathing in his scent. Lashes lifted and dark eyes looked into his. His breath lodged in his throat. *Madre del Dio.* He couldn't help himself. He *had* to kiss her again.

Eventually he did the right thing, and drove her the short distance off the Cape to Signora Mancini's. So why did it feel so much like the *wrong* thing?

'I don't want to leave you here,' he complained, linking his fingers with hers as they walked hand in hand to the front door.

'Signora Mancini will be worried. I need to speak to her about Nonna, and to settle up for our stay—I promised her I would be here. And I have the packing to do.'

Seb was disappointed, but he knew Gina's mind was made up. 'If you are sure that is what you want. But you will promise me one thing,' he demanded, turning her to face him, noting that her lips were still plump from his kisses.

'What is it?'

'You will phone or text me at any time of the night if you want to talk or you want me to come and pick you up?'

For a moment she hesitated. 'I—'

'Promise me, Gina,' he insisted, and his urgency, his need, must have registered, because a sweet, understanding smile gentled her expression, and the palm of her free hand brushed soothingly across his face.

'Yes. I promise.'

'Thank you.'

'Thank *you*,' she stressed. 'For today, for Nonna...for everything.'

He cupped her cheek, needing to feel her silken skin against his own. 'There is nothing to thank me for. I will do anything I can for you, and for Maria.'

'Seb...'

She reached up to kiss him, and he had to force himself to release her. 'Go. Before I change my mind. I will be here to collect you first thing in the morning.'

'Tomorrow,' she whispered with throaty promise.

His gaze clashed with hers. Electric tension sizzled between them...and then the door closed softly, with him on the wrong side of it. For a moment he rested a palm against the solid wooden barrier, the caveman in him wanting to break it down to get to Gina. Then he turned restlessly away and headed home, certain neither of them would sleep that night.

Their sensual chemistry and magnetic connection had left them suspended on the cusp of something extraordinary—scary and wonderfully exciting. He could only hope that tomorrow Gina would make her decision, and they would explore and discover the extent of their combined passion.

CHAPTER SIX

EVERYTHING had gone according to plan, Gina acknowledged with a satisfied smile, sitting for a moment beside the bed as her grandmother, settled and contented at the villa, enjoyed an afternoon nap, propped up on pillows to ease her breathing.

After enduring a sleepless night, cursing herself for being all kinds of a fool for spending it alone, Gina had been thankful to welcome Seb's obscenely early arrival that morning. From the look of him, his night had been no more restful than hers. His urgent, demanding kiss in greeting had robbed her of breath and set her pulse racing.

Having said farewell to Signora Mancini, and moved the luggage to the villa, they had returned to Portoferraio and the hospital, where Gina had been delighted to discover her grandmother had enjoyed a peaceful night and was feeling considerably better. Dottore Vasari had been more than happy to discharge her to their care. A stop at a pharmacy in town to fill the prescription he'd given had followed, which had allowed Gina to buy some things she wanted for Seb, while pretending not to notice as he purchased condoms. She had been crazy with anticipation as it was. Now she was wound up tighter than a bowstring.

She wasn't sure when she had made the final decision to go for what she wanted and take this chemistry she shared with Seb to its natural conclusion. Her grandmother had encouraged her to grasp happiness when it came her way, not to be scared to acknowledge her feelings. Was this how the older woman had felt fifty years ago, meeting Matthew? All Gina knew was that Seb had changed her, awoken her, made her feel alive, special, confident in herself as a desirable woman. Elba's magic combined with the warmth of Seb's romancing of her made her feel free to explore the side of her she had ignored for years. Yes, it had happened quickly, but the way she felt about Seb was far from casual. Desire had grown to so much more.

Now, leaving her grandmother to sleep, Gina collected the bag of items she had bought that morning and went in search of Seb, finding him in the villa's airy living room. Sitting on an expensive leather sofa, a sports magazine discarded beside him, he had a frown on his face as he flexed his right hand. Gina hesitated, her nerves tightening as she wondered how to broach the subject of his injuries. As if sensing her presence, he looked up, and a smile chased away the frown.

'How is Maria?'

'She's settled and asleep. Her breathing sounds much better,' Gina informed him, stepping closer, aware of the edgy tension between them. Taking a deep breath, she sank to her knees in front of him and set down her bag. Gently, she took his right hand in hers. 'May I? Please?'

For a moment she felt his resistance, but although he remained wary, his expression guarded, he nodded. Struck by the strength of his hand in hers, the feel of his skin, smooth and supple but slightly coarser than her own, she tried to ignore her body's reaction, her awareness and shiver of desire. Opening the bag, she took a moment to prepare the things she had selected for him.

'Gina, what are you doing?' he queried, his uncertainty evident.

'I bought some essential oils,' she explained, concentrating on her task, mixing them with a base oil and then pouring some into her palms to warm it before taking his hand again. 'I'm using chamomile and lavender, both of which have anti-inflammatory and soothing properties. The carrier oil is calendula, which has anti-inflammatory and antispasmodic properties, vitamins, and is also good for healing wounds and bruising.'

As she talked, she carefully began a light, gentle massage of his right hand, paying special attention to the areas affected by the slashing cuts across his wrist, palm and the mound at the base of his thumb. She knew this was where he experienced most sensory and motor problems, with discomfort, tingling and locking in his thumb and forefinger. After several minutes she took some more oil and switched to his left arm, working down from the scar by his inner elbow to where some numbness lingered along the side of his hand and into his little finger.

The aroma of the oils scented the air around them, and she heard his breathing change as some of the anxiety drained out of him. She was far from relaxed herself, struggling to focus on her task and not on the sensuousness of gliding her fingers over his bronzed olive skin. Appreciating the benefits of massage and essential oils, she had done this often before, for her grandmother and for friends, male and female. *Never* had it affected her like this. Biting her lip, she shifted restlessly, returning her attention to Seb's more troublesome right hand, using the pads of her thumbs to work gently across his palm and into the heel and wrist.

'Gina.'

Seb's smoky voice vibrated along her nerve-endings. Looking up, she met his gaze, saw the fire in his eyes, the consuming desire. She couldn't breathe. Her heart was thudding. She felt warm and buzzingly alive. Then his fingers closed around hers, his left hand cupping her cheek as he drew her closer, his lips parting as they captured hers in a slow, thorough kiss. *Oh, my!* But just as she was losing herself in Seb's magic touch and taste, they were disturbed by the sound of the front door closing and someone calling his name.

'Dannazione!'

Cursing the interruption, Seb reluctantly released Gina and moved away, giving her a moment to compose herself. She had taken him by surprise with the essential oils, and her bold insistence on confronting his injuries head-on. When she had begun the massage he had been doubtful about its effects, but he couldn't deny how good it had felt. Whether that was just her touch, or whether the oils really worked, he couldn't say—and he had no more time to ponder on it, as Evelina Gilletti bustled into the room.

Short and rotund, with curly salt-and-pepper hair, the sixty-year-old had been part of the villa for as long as Seb could remember. She lived locally with her vast family, had a kind heart and a ready smile, and, despite her propensity to talk incessantly, she was the soul of discretion. She came in a couple of days a week to clean when any of the family were on the island, and checked up on things every day when the villa was empty. Knowing Evelina would be anxious to help, and the perfect person to keep an eye on Maria should he and Gina want to go out or have some time alone, he had phoned to brief her the night before.

'Evelina, how are you?' he asked in Italian, because her English was limited.

'I am good, thank you.' She glanced past him, brown eyes twinkling with mischief as she studied Gina with curiosity. 'You must introduce me, Sebastiano.'

Evelina was one of the few people who got away with calling him by his full name. He just hoped she would remember his request of the night before and not make any comments to Gina or Maria about who he was. Giving her a warning frown, he introduced her to Gina, thankful that the two very different women took to each other from the first and chatted comfortably…or rather Gina listened with a smile as Evelina talked twenty to the dozen.

'Gina, I thought that Evelina would be able to keep Maria company sometimes,' Seb said, when he could get a word in, explaining the woman's position at the villa.

'That would be very kind. I am sure Nonna will enjoy that. Are you sure it is no bother?'

Evelina gave a dismissive wave of her hand. 'But of course not! Your grandmother and I will have a fine time discussing Elba and life in general. How is she feeling?'

'She is much better. In fact, she's having a nap at the moment,' Gina informed her, and Seb was relived to see that the anxiety shadowing her eyes had vanished now Maria was out of hospital.

'*Bene*. You young ones must go off and enjoy yourselves,' Evelina insisted. 'I will be here for Maria. And I will prepare something for you all to eat later.'

Keen to have Gina to himself, Seb was happy to agree. 'A good idea. Gina, we shall go to the beach for a swim, yes?'

'Yes.' A tinge of pink stained her cheeks as her gaze darted to his and away again. 'I'll get my things. Thank you, Evelina.'

Seb went to his room to change into swim shorts and collect a towel, waiting impatiently for Gina to join him. He could still taste her. Every touch, every kiss increased the tension between them—the last days had been a lingering foreplay that was going to rage out of control when they couldn't stand the waiting any more.

At last she appeared, fresh-faced, her magnificent hair tied back in a braid, a robe wrapped around her delectable body.

'Ready, *tesoro*?' he asked, reaching for her hand

'Ready.'

The word whispered out of her and carried such a wealth of meaning that he hesitated, his fingers locking with hers as he sought her gaze. The expression in her eyes left him in no doubt that she wanted him as badly as he wanted her.

And that the waiting was becoming too much to bear. His own body tightening in response, he smothered a groan of needy frustration and led her out of the house, away from prying eyes, and across the terrace to the path that marked the way to the cliff steps. He remembered the last time they had been here together...the day they had met—the day he had caught her when she had slipped and he had held her in his arms for the first time.

Keeping hold of her hand, he ensured she was safe on their descent to the private crescent of beach. Once there, he dropped his towel and kicked off his shoes, letting go of her hand as he walked to the water. Turning, he waited for her in the shallows, sensing her moment of shy hesitation before she unfastened the tie of her robe and slowly slid it off her shoulders, allowing it to fall to the ground.

Dio!

His body sprang to instant attention at the sight of her voluptuous curves encased in a red halter-neck bikini. It wasn't skimpy or revealing, but it set off her womanly form to perfection, heated his blood to fever pitch and made his mouth water. His gaze began a leisurely journey up shapely legs to her soft thighs, smooth and golden in the sunshine. For a moment his focus lingered on the red triangle of cloth that hid the heart of her femininity from his view, then he forced himself to move on to the rounded swell of her belly and navel. How sensitive was she there? He wanted to explore *all* of her with his mouth, to seek out all the secret places that would drive her mad with pleasure.

His thought was cut off as he noticed the way Gina lowered her arms to try and cover her belly, as if self-conscious about her body shape. No way was he having that. She was perfect in every respect—something she would be in no doubt about by the time he had thoroughly loved every inch of her.

In the meantime his gaze continued up to the lush fullness of plump breasts, his heart hammering against his ribs as he remembered how it had felt to caress them and taste them last night. He ducked lower in the water, wishing it were several degrees colder to take the edge off his raging desire. Maybe coming to the beach had been a bad idea. He'd thought it might cool them off, but instead he was hotter for her than ever. The temptation of Gina was going to be impossible to resist.

Gina felt Seb's intense gaze on her as she walked the last steps to where he waited for her in the shallows. Her bikini was entirely decent, but she was very aware that he hadn't seen quite so much of her flesh before, and she was anxious she might have a few too many curves and extra pounds for his taste. But, given the flare of hunger in his eyes, maybe he didn't find her too lacking. The self-confidence that had been returning since she had met him expanded inside her, allowing her to acknowledge that Seb liked what he saw, that she was all woman and desired by a sexy man.

The sea was surprisingly warm, and crystal-clear. Once Seb had assured himself that she was a comfortable and competent swimmer, he stroked away from her, as if needing to burn off some excess energy. She knew the feeling. She enjoyed herself in the water, then floated for a while near the rocky outcrop of Neptune's Spear, watching him moving effortlessly back towards her. Her eyes closed briefly as she soaked up the September sunshine, then she started in surprise as Seb's hands closed around her ankles.

His fingers glided slowly up her legs, drawing her with him nearer to the shore, until they were able to stand rib-deep in the water. Her skin quivered from the sure, confident touch of his hands as he helped her upright and urged her closer to him. Droplets of water glistened on his skin, reminding her of the first day she had seen him here. Her sea-god. Neptune was also associated with horses, dolphins and earthquakes, she recalled. Indeed, he was called 'the earthshaker'. Gina thought how apt that was in her own case. Seb had most definitely shaken the very ground beneath her from the second she had seen him, making her feel alive, changing her.

His wet hair was swept back from his face, and a hint of stubble darkened the masculine line of his jaw. Her fingers locked with his. She looked into his eyes, unable to halt the tremor that ran through her at the expression of sultry intent in them seconds before his mouth claimed hers. Her lips parted in welcome, and instantly she was swept away on the now familiar tide of passion that swelled so rapidly between them.

Their kiss deepened and flared out of control. Her hands glided up the corded muscles of his arms and over strong shoulders, until she could wrap her arms around his neck. Seb's hands stroked down her back, cupping the rounded cheeks of her rear, flexing sensuously in her flesh as he rocked her hips with his, making her excitingly aware of his arousal. Her breasts pressed into his chest, the thin bikini no barrier at all, her sensitised nipples grazing against him as their bodies brushed together in the gentle swell of the water. She moaned, trying to get closer, consumed by the potency of his kiss, his taste, his scent. Their tongues teased and twined. As his retreated, hers followed, need spearing through her as he sucked on her, drawing her into his mouth. Every part of her craved more, and she pressed her thighs together in a desperate attempt to ease the ache.

'That won't stop it,' he murmured huskily as his mouth abandoned hers and journeyed around her jaw to her ear, nipping at her lobe before his tongue tormented the hollow beneath. 'Let me help, Gina. I can make you feel so good.'

He wrapped her braid around one wrist, tilting her head to give his seductive mouth better access to her throat as he literally swept her off her feet. As she clung to him for support his other hand glided down her body, lingering to trace teasing circles around her navel before moving on and easing between her thighs. Shamelessly, they parted to give him better access, and she moaned as he cupped her. For a second she tensed, realising where they were.

'Seb…'

Molten caramel eyes looked into hers. 'No one can see, *tesoro*. This is just us.' Bold, clever fingers dipped beneath the waistband of her bikini briefs, creating magic as they explored and caressed.

'Oh, God,' she moaned.

Her breath coming in ragged gasps, she gave herself up to the impossible pleasure of his devastating touch. She had forgotten what this was like…except nothing had been this incredible, nothing had prepared her for the glory of Seb.

When he eased two fingers inside her, unerringly finding the sweetest spot imaginable, he began a rhythmic stroking that threatened to slay her in an instant. Combining that with the teasing, circling rub of his thumb on and around her most sensitive place, Seb sent her straight to paradise. Gina buried her face in his neck, her hands tightening on supple skin and solid muscle, allowing him and the water to support her as she surrendered totally to him and lost herself in exquisite, torturous bliss. Uninhibited, she soared to her release.

Seb drew her head back, watching her face, fiery passion in his eyes. He held her trembling body tightly against him, gentle strokes of his hands slowly easing her down from the incredible pinnacle she had ascended.

Shaking and shaken, she wrapped herself around him. 'It's been so long.' She scarcely realised she had whispered the words aloud as she regained her breath, her heartbeat slowing to its normal rhythm.

She had never felt this amazing, but her release had in no way dimmed her urgent desire for more of Seb. If anything, despite the delicious glow and wonderful languor, her body felt primed and ready. Wanting Seb to feel as good as she did, Gina pulled back a fraction, un-curling her legs from around him. Standing, she saw his surprise and momentary uncertainty as her own hands caressed down his sumptuous body and freed his erection from the confines of his shorts. She loved the feel of him, velvety soft over the hardness, and a moan of excitement escaped as she imagined what it would feel like to make love with him.

'Gina—'

'Please,' she whispered, silencing his warning.

Allowing Gina the same liberties she had granted him, Seb gave himself to the moment. He had never meant things to go this far, but he hadn't been able to stop himself from touching her. She was so incredibly responsive. Watching and feeling her come apart for him had been beautiful. The way she'd reacted so spontaneously to his caresses had excited him, and sparked his imagination about all the different ways to please her. Knowing it had been some time since she had acknowledged the needs of her body and that, like him, she had been on the point of exploding with frustration, he had hoped to take the edge off without spoiling her hunger for later. Now she had turned the tables on him. He should have known. Everything about Gina had been unexpected from the moment he had met her.

His thoughts hazed as his body reacted to her touch. He had never felt this good. *Madre del Dio!* He had no control around this woman. He was already breathless, shaking, tensing, his heart racing, every part of him rushing past the point of no return. She pressed her mouth to his chest, her lips, teeth and tongue caressing his skin, exploring, driving him insane. But not nearly as insane as her hands. Or her throaty murmurs of encouragement as she took him rapidly over the edge, blurring his vision, destroying his reason, making him groan aloud as he was spun into an intense vortex of pleasure.

Afterwards, he hugged her close, and they rolled into the water, soothing overheated skin and trembling bodies. He'd never known anyone like Gina. She was so unselfish, so giving, so sensual. He couldn't wait to know her fully. Never before had he experienced the explosive passion and intensity of need he did with her. But it wasn't just physical lust. There was an over-arching warmth, a deep connection and affection—and a level of trust he had not shared with anyone else. He had only known her a short time, but already she had changed him. He felt a better person when he was with her—happier, more settled, grounded. He couldn't begin to think what life would be like when she left—wouldn't think about it. They had to make the most of every moment.

'I can't wait to make love with you.' He felt a quiver ripple through her at his words. 'I want to explore and devour every inch of you.'

'Seb…'

'I want you, I need you—but only if it's what you want, too,' he told her, his voice low and raw with need, breathing in the scent of vanilla and sea on her damp skin. 'Will you come to me tonight, Gina?'

'Yes.'

The word was torn from her. All too soon it would be time for her to return to the real world, to put the sensual side of her back into hibernation. Whatever the future held after she left this island in a few days' time, she couldn't say no to the magic she and Seb made together. It felt right. He had re-awoken the woman within her, and she craved affection, fulfilment, closeness. She needed this. Most of all she needed Seb…the man who had set her free, who had captured her imagination and, she very much feared, her heart.

They finally made their way off the beach and back up the cliff to the villa. Her grandmother was resting on the terrace, looking both amused and bemused as Evelina chattered at full speed. Gina went to her room to have a bath and get dressed. Every part of her tingled with excitement and anticipation. She wondered how she was going to bear waiting the hours until she could be with Seb.

It proved as difficult as she had imagined. For both of them. Every look, every casual touch ratcheted up the tension and the expectancy until Gina thought she was going to burst out of her skin.

Evelina went home, leaving them to enjoy the meal she had prepared, after which the evening ticked by, each minute passing with agonising slowness. Seb was wonderful with her grandmother, listening to her fondest memories of Elba and meeting Matthew McNaught, and then playing a game of chess with her.

Her heart soared as she watched them together. Seb treated her grandmother with respect, gently teasing her, and under his attention the older lady blossomed, her cheeks pink, laughing with delight for the first time since being widowed. Tears stung Gina's eyes. Seb had given them so much in such a short time. He had given her grandmother hope, his time and his care.

For herself, his gentle touches and small kindnesses, combined with his passionate nature, had made her feel special. She had wondered in the beginning if she could indulge in a holiday fling, but this was so much more. It was no longer about attraction and desire. Her heart was involved. She cared about Seb, felt connected to him in an elemental way, and it was going to be impossible to walk away in a few days' time. But she had never felt anything this incredible before, and she had to live the fantasy while she was here in case she never experienced anything like it again.

'Well, I think it is time I went to bed,' her grandmother announced, and Gina almost jumped out of her chair.

Blushing at the knowing laughter in Seb's eyes, she managed to rise with more decorum, waiting while her grandmother said goodnight to their host. 'I'll come and see you settled, Nonna.'

First she stopped in her own room, wondering what to change into before going to Seb. Just thinking about tonight sent a tremor of excited awareness down her spine. She had nothing to wear, she fretted. The oversized Winnie the Pooh sleep T-shirt Holly had given her for her birthday was hardly alluring! She stifled a giggle, nerves fluttering inside her. The only item of clothing vaguely sexy was the lacy black slip she had worn under her red dress the other night. It would have to do.

Pulling it on, she fastened her robe over the top, then padded barefoot down the corridor to her grandmother's room, finding her already in bed and propped up on the pillows.

'Is there anything I can get for you, Nonna?' she asked, ensuring she was comfortable and had fresh water nearby.

'No, thank you, Gina.' One papery hand cupped her cheek. 'It is good to be here and not in hospital. I am comfortably settled and I feel very well cared for.'

'There's a buzzer beside you if you need to call me for anything in the night.'

Smiling, the older woman tutted. 'You must not worry about me.'

'I can't help it.' Gina gave her a hug and kissed her cheek. 'I love you.'

'I love you, too, my precious girl. You are the most selfless person I have ever known. You give so much of yourself. Now it is your time. It is wonderful to see you so happy—I think Seb is responsible for that, no?' she added, hazel eyes twinkling.

'Yes,' Gina admitted, smiling back.

'Reach for what you want, *ragazza mia*.'

Gina fought back the emotional sting of tears. 'Sleep well, Nonna.'

'I am sure I will.'

For a few moments she sat in the armchair beside the bed, but her grandmother swiftly dozed off, and Gina rose to her feet, content to leave her. Anticipation made her heart race and her legs tremble. She tiptoed from the room and closed the door before turning to walk back down the corridor, and then...

She froze when she saw Seb ahead of her, leaning against the doorway at the end of the guest wing. A towel around his waist was his only covering, and her throat closed as she looked at him—perfect, masculine, breathtakingly gorgeous. Hesitant footsteps carried her closer. Her gaze locked with his, the sultry expression in his eyes making the flames of desire burn ever hotter inside her. He held out his hand, waiting for her. Knowing there was no other decision she was going to make, she placed her hand in his, seeing his sexy smile, the quiet flash of relief as he straightened, then drew her with him out of the guest wing to his own room in the main villa and closed the door.

'You haven't changed your mind, Gina?'

'No.' As if she could. She wanted him more desperately than her next breath. 'You?'

'Never.'

The smile, the promise in his eyes, the certainty of his desire for her, nearly stopped her heart. 'Seb...'

His hands, warm and gentle, cupped her face. 'Nervous?' he asked, surprising her with his understanding.

'A little,' she admitted truthfully. She glanced back towards the door. True, she had her grandmother's blessing, but she still felt a bit awkward. 'I—'

'Do not feel inhibited or embarrassed.' Seb tilted her gaze to his. 'I promise you that Maria will hear nothing.'

She felt reassured—then stupidly wondered how he knew that, if he did this often.

'No.'

'Sorry?' She frowned at him in puzzlement. 'No, what?'

'You were wondering if this is a regular thing for me.'

How did he read her mind like that? 'Seb…'

'The truth is that I have never brought a woman here before. Only you, Gina.'

For a moment she was speechless with surprise, but, looking into his eyes, she believed him. It gave her confidence and courage. 'You know it's been a while for me. I want to be enough for you.'

'*Tesoro*, you are so much more than anyone I have ever known,' he said with a simple sincerity that took her breath away.

He stood behind her and gently unfastened her braid, his fingers combing through the freed waves of her hair with a sensual touch that had her sighing and leaning into him. When he turned her round again she bit her lip as he released the tie holding her robe closed, then she heard his indrawn hiss of breath as he eased it off and his gaze swept over the silky black lace that covered her lush curves.

'You're beautiful, Gina,' he told her hoarsely, drawing her with him as he backed up towards the bed.

She quivered with sensation as his fingertips grazed her thighs and he slowly, slowly drew the slip up her body and over her head before tossing it away, his eyes dark, his breathing uneven as he looked at her, exposed and vulnerable. Her own fingers fumbled with his towel. Releasing it, she let it drop to the floor, running her hands over him, revelling in the texture of his supple skin and the ripple of toned muscle beneath. Her gaze strayed to his impressive arousal, tension coiling inside her. Soon she would know him fully.

Seb's hands explored her with equal thoroughness, driving her insane with wanting. She needed more…so much more. Craved everything. Impatient, she gave him a push, tumbling with him as he fell to the bed, any thought of waiting and teasing gone in the growing urgency of their mutual passion. Despite their sensual play in the sea that afternoon, the days of longing had led them here, and the desperation remained acute. She wriggled on top of him, even more aroused at the rub of her bare skin on his, heat coursing through her at the skilful caress of his hands, their mouths meeting in hungry desire.

Taking advantage of her position, she set off on a journey of exploration, hands and mouth paying homage to his magnificent body. She laved the bronze orbs of his nipples with her tongue before kissing down to his navel, allowing the fall of her hair to caress him. He shifted restlessly beneath her, his muscles tautening, the ardent press of his arousal exciting her.

'Not this time, Gina.' His voice was low and raw as he caught her arms and pulled her back up, giving her a short but very sexy kiss. 'I'm too close to the edge. I need you so badly.'

'Me, too.'

She gave him room to reach for the drawer in the bedside chest, watching as he took out the bag he had brought from the pharmacy that morning. He tipped it up, catching one of the boxes and impatiently tossing the other aside. Filled with unbearable urgency, she took the box from him, wrestling with the outer wrapper, tremors running through her as his hands stroked her heated, sensitised body. Finally she managed to extract a foil packet. Opening it, she evaded him and skimmed down to roll it on, her fingers lingering to caress him.

'Enough,' he groaned, rolling them over, settling her under him and fanning her hair out on the pillows.

Never had she felt so desired, so wanted, so cherished, as Seb's kisses and caresses brought her to a new fever-pitch of need. She sank her hands into his hair, arching to him as his mouth worked its magic on her breasts, drawing each nipple in turn deep inside and suckling strongly, spearing sensation straight to her womb. On fire, desperate to assuage the terrible empty ache within her, she writhed beneath him, inviting, begging, pleading. She needed release *now* and yet she wanted the most incredible experience of her life to last for ever.

'Seb, please,' she demanded, pressing her pelvis to his, rubbing her softness against his hardness.

His fingertips grazed up her thighs, tormenting her, and she wrapped her legs around him in blatant encouragement. Catching both her hands in one of his, he pinned them above her head, setting his mouth to the hollow of her throat where her pulse rampaged wildy.

'Gina, I want to explore you, savour you, love you for hours. But I am too impatient to wait now.'

'I don't want you to wait!' She couldn't last another second.

He buried his free hand in her hair, eyes dark and fiery with passion as he held her gaze. 'We'll slow down—next time we'll do this properly,' he promised roughly, moving against her, uniting them with one searing motion.

Gina gasped at the blissful wonder of being joined completely with Seb. This wasn't *properly*? She had never felt anything so shatteringly beautiful. His body filled hers almost beyond bearing. It was incredible. Perfect. Frantic, immediate and amazing. She wanted everything.

Freeing her hands, she moved them over his back, instinctively meeting and matching his moves, her body totally in tune with his. The delicious friction and sense of impossible fullness as they moved together was mind-blowing. Wave after wave of ecstasy built inside her. Her heart thundered, her lungs were on the point of bursting, but she wanted more, needed everything, couldn't bear for this to ever stop. She pressed her face into his shoulder, breathing in his seductive scent, tasting his warm flesh. She'd forgotten what it was like…and yet it had never, ever been like this.

Seb praised her in Italian, telling her how beautiful she was, how unbelievable she felt, urging her on, taking more, giving everything in return. She relished their blaze of passion. The searing rhythm rushed them both to the point of no return. Drawing her legs higher, she opened more to him, crying out as he sank deeper still, his free arm curling under her hips to keep her tight to him. The pressure was so intense she couldn't stand it.

'Now, Seb. Please.'

His hand in her hair fisted, his breath hot on her neck, his mouth urgent as he bit and sucked at her skin. 'Now.'

Together they soared off the precipice, swirling into oblivion. She feared she might faint from the sheer ecstatic pleasure of it. Sobbing, she clung to him as he masterfully extended and prolonged her shattering climax, binding her to him as he rode out his own. She had no idea where she ended and he began. They were one, sharing something so intense, so incredible, she wasn't sure she would survive it.

They collapsed together, gasping for breath, hearts thundering. Every part of her was shaking, and ripples of sensation continued to undulate through her. Rolling them to the side, Seb drew her leg over his hip and held her close. She felt the tremor in his hands as he gentled her, his fingertips brushing the tears from her cheeks.

'You are mine, Gina *mia*. Mine,' Seb proclaimed over and over, possessive, determined. '*Sempre*…always.'

Wrapping her arms around him, burying her face in his neck, she never wanted to let him go.

Seb had never experienced anything so incredible in his life as the storm of desire he had shared with Gina. He had no idea how much time passed in a haze of fulfilment until some semblance of normal thought processes were possible again. He nuzzled closer to her. The scent of vanilla clung to her skin, the familiar aroma mingling with her own unique womanliness—warm, sexy and intensely arousing. Just a short while ago he hadn't thought he would ever be able to move again, but he was gaining a second wind, and he needed to kiss her, explore her, taste her…do all the things he had not done properly the first time as they gave themselves to the urgent demands of their passion.

'Don't go.'

Gina's husky protest came as he eased her onto her back and tucked a pillow more comfortably under her head. He had no intention of going anywhere—as she would soon discover. Taking a moment to enjoy the way her hair tumbled around her, unrestrained and luxuriant, he knelt back, smiling as he looked her over. A smile of possession. Because spread out beneath him, eyes closed and skin flushed, she looked the picture of abandonment…a woman completely and thoroughly satisfied.

His woman.

Needing to touch her, he ran one palm slowly from her throat, down the valley between her delectable breasts, over her navel—noting how her stomach muscles spasmed in reaction—then lower, to rub his fingers back and forth just above her pubic bone. He added enough pressure to have her arching beneath him, giving a throaty moan of pleasure. Sooty lashes fluttered open to reveal dark, slumberous eyes.

He leaned down to kiss her. 'Hi.'

'Hi.' She skimmed her fingers along his forearms, her breath catching as he worked his mouth down her throat and licked his way to her breasts. 'Seb…'

'Mmm?'

'I can't yet,' she protested half-heartedly, making him chuckle because her body was betraying her and responding to his touch, her nipples swelling and tautening.

'You can.' Reluctantly relinquishing one delicious prize, he whispered his lips down to her navel, loving the way she moaned and bowed into him as he kissed, licked and sucked on her skin. 'I intend to do all the work this time.'

Starting at her feet, he continued his journey of discovery, leaving not a fragment of her untouched or unexplored,

finding and exploiting the places where she was most sensitive, learning what made her come apart, where and how
she most loved to be touched. He inched his way all over
her until finally settling himself between her thighs, his
hands curling over her hips and belly as she writhed
beneath him, whimpering as he set his mouth to the core
of her femininity, relishing her taste, her uninhibited and
instinctive reactions to his caresses.

'Seb!' She shifted restlessly, clutching at him as he took
her up a plateau at a time, then kept her balanced precariously on the edge of release. 'Please!'

'Patience, *amore mia.*'

He teased her, drawing out the delicious torture until she
was crazy with need, before allowing her to crash over the
edge, holding her close as she spun through the vortex of
pleasure. And then he started all over again, welcoming her
eager participation as she gave back just as readily and
explored him with equal endeavour.

It was a very long time later when they finally fell into
an exhausted, sated sleep, locked in each other's arms.

Seb woke with a feeling of incredible contentment. Gina
was spooned against him, and his arms were closed pos-
sessively around her. For a man who had never before
brought a woman to his home or his bed, who had never
spent the whole night with a woman, he had made a remark-
able discovery in the last hours. He could not now imagine
ever sleeping another night without Gina in his arms.

Brushing her hair back, curling the silken mass up on
the pillow, he softly moved his lips over the back of her
neck, careful not to wake her. He smothered a sigh, horribly
aware that he had still not told her the full truth about
himself. The more he knew her, the more he cared about
her, and the harder it was to own up, to risk ruining the most
special thing he had ever experienced.

She was the most amazing woman. Incredibly responsive and receptive to his touch, she gave herself so generously, abandoned and without inhibition. The hours learning her body had been blissful, discovering her most sensitive places…the insides of her thighs, her navel, her breasts, the hollows below her ears, the backs of her knees, the base of her spine near the tattoo. He had discovered how to send her straight to orbit, and how to keep her on the edge of pleasure for ages. He loved it. Loved everything about her, every part of her. Loved nothing more than pleasuring her. It wasn't sex. It was making love.

And it hit him. No way were a few days and nights going to be enough. In a short time Gina had changed him—opened his eyes, given him hope, a sense of purpose for his future. His injuries had brought him to Elba. Elba had brought him Gina. And Gina had given him back his own reality and sense of self. He was angry at the way he had wasted his surgical skill, angry at what felt like the temporary loss of his very soul, sacrificed on the fake altar of money and success. He didn't like the person he had been, the kind of doctor he had become, but Gina had led him out of the darkness and into the light.

Maybe the new life ahead opened the way for him to have a proper relationship—the chance to make a real commitment to something other than his job. Not long ago such thoughts would have scared him. Now he was filled with an increasing excitement and awareness that Gina could be *the one*. All he knew was that he couldn't let her go. Which meant that somehow he would have to stop her leaving…or go with her.

He had no idea about her feelings. He could only hope this meant something to her. At some point they needed to have a serious talk. Knowing how important Gina's nursing was to her, Seb would not insult her by suggesting she give it up. True, he had enough money that neither of them needed to worry much about work again—not that she knew that yet. But he could never sit back and do nothing, and he knew Gina would feel the same.

Sighing, he glanced at the clock, surprised at how late they had slept. He needed to check on Maria. And it wouldn't be long before Evelina arrived. With regret, he gently eased away from Gina, tucking the covers around her and leaving her to catch up on some of the sleep he had denied her through their long night of loving.

He had two main problems to solve and answers to find...

What was he going to do with the rest of his life?

And how would Gina react when she knew the full story about him?

CHAPTER SEVEN

'NONNA, are you all right?' Gina asked, watching her grandmother stand on the harbourside at Marciana Marina and gaze out to sea, as if miles away in the past.

She turned and offered a teary smile, one that pulled at Gina's heartstrings. 'I am just feeling sentimental. Remembering.'

'Oh, Nonna.' She slipped an arm around her frail shoulders. It was the third morning of their stay at the villa, and although her health had improved rapidly since leaving hospital, Gina couldn't help but worry. 'Are you sure you're up to this?'

'It was always going to be emotional.'

'I know, but…' Gina paused, biting her lip in indecision, looking across to where middle-aged, balding Paolo Benigni, a former fisherman who now ran chartered boat trips, was talking to Seb. 'You can change your mind at any time.'

Her grandmother shook her head. 'This is right, Gina. I must do it—I *want* to do it.'

'OK.'

'It is time to do what we came here for…time things went full circle.' One frail hand cupped her cheek. 'Do not be sad, *ragazza mia*. It is the way of life. Think of all the happy years. Were it not for the life I have been blessed with—including having you as part of it—I would not be here at all.'

Blinking back tears, Gina let out a shaky breath, keeping her misgivings to herself. A lump in her throat, she struggled to come to terms with what was about to happen. Yes, this was the reason they had come to Elba, and she supported her grandmother, had promised to carry out her grandparents' wishes, but… She closed her eyes. It was still hard to let go, to face saying goodbye again to the grandfather she'd loved so much.

'There is a heavy storm coming later in the day,' Seb announced, coming up beside them. 'Paolo says we need to go now…if we're going.'

'We are going,' her grandmother stated with her customary determination.

Gina managed a shaky smile as Seb glanced at her, then turned away. 'Come, Maria. Let me help you.'

Together, Seb and Paolo guided her grandmother on board the boat and saw her comfortably settled, the precious urn clasped protectively in her lap. Gina tossed her braid over her shoulder and looked away, needing a moment to get her emotions in check. Familiar hands settled on her shoulders, thumbs caressing the nape of her neck, and Gina turned, wrapping her arms around Seb's waist, pressing her face against him. One of his hands rubbed her back, and the other cradled her head as he gave her the comfort she needed, letting her absorb his strength.

'How are you doing?'

'I'm fine,' she fibbed, feeling selfish for her doubts and reluctance when this was what her grandparents had planned and so desperately wanted.

She burrowed more fully into his embrace and turned her thoughts to him. The last days with Seb had been the happiest of her life. And the nights had been incredible. They had quickly fallen into a comfortable routine. The three of them would spend their mornings on short sightseeing trips, with Seb an entertaining and patient escort. Then after lunch Evelina would come to the villa and keep a resting Maria company while Gina went out with Seb, walking or cycling in the national park, exploring the island or swimming at the private cove.

The previous afternoon they had visited an old mine and its museum, where Seb had bought her a glorious piece of mineral, a classic example of the 'Elbaite' commonly found on the island. The subtle colours and shapes in the smoky quartz with its pieces of tourmaline and beryl intrigued her, and she would cherish it always.

In the evenings, after Evelina had gone home, the three of them ate together, then relaxed until her grandmother went to bed. Then it was time for her and Seb to be alone, to explore the passion that only seemed to burn hotter between them.

Gina shivered in reaction as she thought of those nights with him. Seb was an amazing lover. Intensely sexy, he seemed to know even before she did what her body needed—how to maximise and prolong her pleasure. He was demanding and hungry, but incredibly generous. Sometimes she thought she would expire as he devoted hours to her pleasure, teasing and tormenting her until she couldn't bear it another moment. At other times it was hot, wild, excitingly rough as they gave in to their raging desire. Seb was full of contrasts, adventurous and deliciously naughty. Being with him was the most fantastic experience of her life.

Seb had set her free, releasing the sensual side she'd kept hidden…not that she had ever been as alive and uninhibited with anyone as she was with him. She'd surrendered to him totally, her body glowing and humming from his lovemaking. All she could think about was being with him. She craved his touch, the unbelievable sense of fullness and rightness as she welcomed him inside her, the indescribable pleasure only he had ever given her. His own body was exquisite, and she enjoyed every opportunity of exploring him and bringing him pleasure in return.

'Ready to go?'

His question cut through her reverie and she drew back

with a sigh. 'Yes. Let's do it,' she agreed, hoping she sounded more certain and together than she felt.

On the journey west, around the coast and back towards the villa's secluded cove on Capo Sant'Andrea, Seb chatted to her grandmother. But Gina was grateful for the comfort and support of his fingers curled with hers.

All too soon they arrived at their destination. Paolo was discretion itself and he gave them privacy, ducking below while Seb assisted her grandmother.

'What do you want to do, Maria?' he asked, helping her to stand and steadying her on the gently swaying deck. 'Do you need to be nearer the shore? Or do you wish to scatter Matthew's ashes here, by Neptune's Spear?'

'I had meant to go to the beach, but I think the water would be a lovely idea—given my Matteo's love of the sea,' her grandmother decided, her voice shaky with emotion, tears shimmering in her eyes.

Gina had to struggle to hold back her own. 'Are you sure, Nonna?'

'Yes, *ragazza mia*, I am.'

'Whatever you want,' she conceded.

She felt choked as her grandmother made a short but emotional speech about meeting her true love here and their love together. Then Seb helped her to the side of the boat. The breeze was behind her as she uncapped the urn and tilted it, the ashes floating away on the water.

'I want to come here, too, when my time comes.' Cheeks moist, but her expression determined, her grandmother faced her. 'Promise me, Gina.'

'I promise, Nonna.'

Gina barely got the words out before she had to turn away again, the tears she had tried so hard to hide now escaping. It was difficult enough being here to say goodbye to her grandfather, the man she had loved and admired so much. She couldn't bear to think of repeating this in time to come for her grandmother.

Seb came up behind her, one arm wrapping around her waist, one around her shoulders, cocooning her in his warmth. She leaned back against him and he pressed a kiss to her temple, giving her strength and comfort without voicing any unwanted platitudes. There was nothing anyone could say to make this easier to bear. It was enough that he understood, that he gave her his support.

With the wind picking up and the sea turning choppy, the atmosphere increasingly thick and airless, it was time to head back to the harbour. Paolo was respectful, maintaining silence as he guided the boat towards Marciana Marina. Gina glanced at her grandmother. She looked pale and tired, but she exuded a peaceful serenity that implied this had, indeed, been the right thing for her to do.

Back at the port, Gina walked down the gangway and watched as Seb and Paolo aided her grandmother safely to the shore.

'Thank you for all you have done for us.' Gina shook Paolo's hand in gratitude. 'I really appreciate you helping my grandmother like this.'

'It is my honour to assist, *signorina*. Besides, my family owe Seb a huge debt after all he did for our daughter,' he announced, taking her by surprise.

'Paolo.'

Gina heard the warning in Seb's voice, but was unable to decipher the silent message that passed between the two men. Curious, she bit back her questions...for now. They said their goodbyes, leaving Paolo to secure his boat to ride out the coming storm.

Back at the villa, her grandmother went to her room to replace the now empty urn and have a quiet moment alone before lunch, while Gina followed Seb to the kitchen.

'Thank you again for what you did today, Seb.'

'I promised,' he replied simply. 'It was what Maria needed... But it upset you, and for that I am sorry.'

'It was what my grandparents wanted.' She paused a

moment, thinking of all that had happened in a few short days. 'I wish I could thank the Linardis for their help and hospitality.'

Seb looked awkward. 'They would not have had it any other way.'

Gina remained silent for a few moments, uncertain whether to press him further. Then she remembered what had happened when they had come off the boat.

'What did you do for Paolo's daughter?' The words bubbled free, and she saw Seb stiffen, his back to her as he opened the fridge and took out some fresh fruit juice. 'Seb?'

'It was nothing, Gina,' he excused, clearly uncomfortable.

'Paolo doesn't think so.'

Pouring two glasses, he pushed one across the counter towards her. 'His child had an accident. I just happened to be in the right place at the right time.'

His tone told her that the subject was closed. A flicker of unease rippled through her, one she couldn't explain, but shadows darkened Seb's eyes and she knew something was troubling him. Something he refused to discuss with her. It hurt to be shut out. And it made her realise how little she knew about him and his life, despite their intimacy...an intimacy that, for her, had gone far beyond the physical.

Before she could try to find out more, her grandmother joined them in the kitchen and the moment was lost.

The predicted storm hit the island during the afternoon. Torrential rain kept them inside the villa. Thunder rocked and rumbled across a blackened sky, streaks of lightning casting unpredictable flashes in the unnatural darkness, the wind battering the trees and threatening to carry off anything not well anchored down. But the freak weather passed within hours, leaving the air clearer and fresher, fragranced with the warm dampness of the earth, and the foliage glistening and beaded under the moonlight.

After she saw her grandmother settled later that night, Gina went out onto the terrace, alone for a few moments with her thoughts. Niggling doubts and unasked questions continued to prey on her mind. Her grandmother spoke romantically of history repeating itself, of Gina meeting Seb on the same spot where her grandparents had found each other fifty years ago. But could she trust her feelings, the speed of it, the fairytale nature of what had happened these last days? What of the things she didn't know about Seb? Why was he so reluctant to talk about himself?

It had been an emotional day. Maria had retired earlier than usual, and Seb stopped off to see her, anxious to ensure that she was not suffering any reaction. He tapped on the door of her room.

'I am awake.'

Smiling, he went inside, pleased to see good colour in her cheeks as she rested against the pillows. '*Buonasera*, Maria. I wanted to check that you were all right.'

'Seb, *buonasera*!' she greeted him, patting the bed and waiting for him to sit down beside her. 'Thank you for thinking of me, and for all you have done for me. I am very grateful.'

'I was glad to be able to help. It was obvious how important it was for you to lay Matthew to rest here. But it can't have been easy,' he acknowledged, taking her hand.

'No. Not easy. Yet now it is done I feel a real peace and rightness.' Hazel eyes shimmered with tears, but her smile was strong. 'Wherever I go, whatever happens, my Matteo will always be with me.'

Seb found himself uncharacteristically affected by the depth of Maria's love and inner contentment. 'You are a very special lady.'

'A lucky one, I think, for having lived a happy life. Today I was more worried for Gina than for myself,' she continued after a moment's pause, her smile fading. 'She has supported me always, but I know this was hard for her. Her grandfather meant the world to her.'

'As do you,' Seb pointed out, continually struck by the deep relationship the two women shared.

'For Matteo and me, Gina has been a joy. We have always been proud of her. I don't know what we would have done without her. But I worry she takes on so much responsibility for me, feels she has to protect me. I know money is more of a problem than she will admit, that she struggled to get us here at all, and I know that she goes without things for herself to make sure I am comfortable.'

'Gina loves you.'

Maria's smile was wide and warm. 'I know. And I love her. But I don't want her giving up her own life for me. She hasn't dated at all since we went to live with her.'

Yet Gina had come to him with a freshness, honesty and eagerness that continued to take his breath away, blooming like a flower feeling the heat of the sun after a long winter.

'You are very professional doing that, Seb.'

Maria's words hit home, and he looked at her in confusion. 'Sorry?'

'You're taking my pulse. Gina does the same thing all the time and she thinks I don't know,' she confided with a teasing smile.

Startled, Seb glanced down, realising that unconscious force of habit had indeed led him to do as Maria claimed. 'I—' He broke off, unsure what to say, but as he went to remove his hand, Maria's fingers closed around his.

'A little advice from an old woman. Do not leave it too long to tell Gina whatever you need to.'

'Maria…'

'You are not simply the caretaker of this villa, are you? Or an artist?' she asked softly, and there was no judgement in her tone, just understanding and gentleness.

Seb sighed, unable to tell her anything but the truth. 'No.'

'I'm sure you have your reasons for keeping things to yourself.'

'I did. In the beginning,' he admitted, running a hand

through his hair in agitation. 'Now things have just become complicated, and that's my fault.'

Maria patted his hand. 'I believe you care very much for my Gina.'

'I do. For the first time in my life I've met someone who sees the me inside, Maria. The real person, not the outer trappings.' He hesitated, trying to put his feelings into words. 'I am scared that what I have to say will change how Gina feels about me, that she will judge me harshly and find me wanting.'

'As you do yourself?' she queried with stunning perception.

'Yes.' Taken aback, he looked away, unable to meet her gaze. His own fell on the scars on his right wrist and hand where Maria's fingers rested. 'Meeting Gina has caused me to re-evaluate things and see where I was going wrong. Now I have to decide how to put things right...with her and my life.'

'I know her, Seb, and I have never seen her so happy as when she is with you. My heart tells me you belong together.' A note of warning crept into her voice. 'Gina has a big capacity for understanding and for compassion—but she does value honesty. Whatever it is you are holding back, it will be better coming from you. Tell her yourself—soon.'

He nodded, but Maria's words filled him with anxiety. She was right, but that didn't make telling Gina any easier. How much time did he have left? Now that Maria was well enough to travel, and they had achieved what they had came to Elba to do, what more was there to keep them on the island? They were booked to return to Scotland in a couple of days, and Gina would be starting her new job the following week—unless he faced up to the truth and devised an alternative plan. Never before had he allowed himself to need anyone, to trust and depend on anyone but himself. He had even kept a part of himself detached from Zio Roberto, Zia Sofia and Rico. In an impossibly short time Gina had come to be as important and essential to his very existence as air and water. He couldn't let her walk out of his life— but would she want him when she knew the truth?

'Think on what I have said,' Maria advised now.

'I will. Thank you.' Full of affection for the elderly lady, he leaned down and kissed her cheek before rising to his feet. 'Is there anything I can get for you?'

'No, I'll be fine, *caro. Buonanotte.*'

'Goodnight, Maria. Sleep well.'

Troubled by his thoughts, he left Maria's room, returning to his own to make a few preparations before going in search of Gina. He was uncomfortably aware that he hadn't handled things well earlier, that he had upset her by cutting off her understandable questions. But he hadn't wanted to talk about Paolo's daughter. That would have meant explaining the corrective surgery he had performed for free on the little girl after her nasty accident…and how could he do that when he had still not told Gina about his former career?

Maria's advice and her blessing of their relationship took root inside him. He knew what he had to do. Tonight he would show Gina in every way he could how much she meant to him. Tomorrow he would sit her down and tell her everything.

'What are you thinking, *amore mia*?'

Gina stifled a gasp of surprise, a tremor running through her as Seb moved up behind her and wrapped his arms around her, nuzzling into her, his lips, teeth and tongue tormenting her lobe and the hollow below her ear. Her body reacted instinctively the moment he touched her. It was hard to believe that anything else mattered when he made her feel like this, devoting himself to her pleasure, cherishing her as no one else had ever done.

'Nothing,' she whispered, unable to voice her nagging worries about the way he evaded talking about himself.

It was magical here, and she was caught up in the

romance of the island. The enchantment of being with Seb, his nearness, was affecting her powers of thought and her concentration.

'Come, Gina, I have a treat for you.'

She allowed him to lead her indoors, finding a bubble bath awaiting her, with scented candles casting their flickering light around the room. His thoughtfulness touched her. Her physical need of him obliterated the unasked questions in her mind, and her fingers went to work dispensing with his clothes, as his did with hers. After she had wound her braid into a knot and pinned it up, he took her hand, balancing her as she stepped into the large corner tub. With a contented sigh, she sank down into the water, making room for Seb to join her before resting back against his chest, sighing as he nibbled the back of her neck. He took the soap, his hands enjoying a leisurely journey over her body before allowing her to turn and do the same for him.

A while later, her skin tingling and her pulse scudding through her veins, they were out of the bath and patted dry. Then Seb surprised her again, leading her naked to the bed and spreading out a dry towel.

'Lie face down for me,' he instructed huskily.

Trembling with anticipation, she did as she was bid. The bed depressed under his weight as he knelt over her, straddling her thighs. His body brushed against her as he leaned down and kissed the back of her neck, before running lips and tongue slowly down her spine to linger over her tattoo. She shivered in reaction. When contact was withdrawn and he paused, she turned her head on the pillow to see what he was doing.

'Seb?'

'I borrowed some of your oils,' he told her, reaching out to a bowl on the bedside chest and pouring some of the contents into his palm.

'That's fine.' She had been massaging his hands and arm every day. The thought that he was now going to reciprocate—all over—made her body hum with feverish expectancy. As she had already discovered, he had amazing hands. A subtle waft of her favourite fragrance stirred her senses. 'Vanilla…'

Moving back into position, he leaned down again, making her squirm as he sucked her earlobe into his mouth. 'It always makes me think of you…makes me hot and needy.' His voice was a rough, sexy murmur, and he deliberately rubbed himself against her, letting her feel his arousal before he moved away again.

'Seb…'

His hands settled on her back and began to glide over her with just the right pressure, the sensuous strokes making her sigh with pleasure. When his thumbs sank into the cheeks of her rear and set up a circular rhythm it was so unexpectedly arousing that she buried her face in the pillow to smother her moans. He moved on, journeying down each leg in turn, and she wriggled as he hit the most sensitive spots, hearing him chuckle as he lingered to torment her.

'Turn over, *amore mia.*'

Wicked fingertips tickling the soles of her feet made her hasten to comply with the demand. Gentle light spilled across the bed, allowing her to see the raw desire in Seb's eyes as he looked at her, and she sucked in a breath, not sure she was going to survive whatever else he had planned for her. All she could focus on was Seb, and how amazing he made her feel. She wanted him…*now*.

'You are so beautiful,' he whispered, the emotion in his voice almost making her heart stop. His reverential appreciation of her made her feel supremely confident in her power as a woman—a power only Seb had given her.

Taking more oil, he started at her feet, driving her insane as he worked slowly up her legs, skimming the insides of her thighs but stopping short of where she most craved his touch. His knee between hers prevented her pressing her legs together to try and stop the terrible ache of need building inside her. Then his hands moved on to stroke and massage her belly, circling her navel, dipping to press just above her pubic bone, making her hips lift in involuntary response, begging him to fill the emptiness.

'Please,' she whimpered.

'Soon.'

Her protest was choked off as he turned his attention to her breasts, his firm, clever caresses almost too much to bear. Her muscles felt boneless, relaxed, yet her body was wound up like at top. There was no way she could wait any more. Sitting up, she caught him by surprise, and he laughed, his arms closing round her as she tumbled him to the bed and settled on top of him. His mouth opened hotly under hers as she kissed him with all the pent-up desperation coursing through veins.

'Are you that hungry?' he teased, fingers skimming her heated, trembling flesh.

'Yes.'

The fire in his own eyes matched that which burned inside her as he reached out for a condom and handed it to her. 'Then take what you need, Gina. I am all yours.'

How she wished that were true—at least beyond this moment. She knew without doubt that she loved him. But she didn't know what he felt—if anything. In a couple of days she and her grandmother were due to go home. She couldn't bear the thought of saying goodbye to him...knew that when she did she would never see him again. As much as she loved her grandmother, her friends and her work, home would mean responsibility, an end to the freedom and romance she had found here. Seb was the only one with the key to unlock the sensual woman inside her.

Unable to say the words aloud, she gave everything to show with her body what he meant to her.

Seb let Gina take the lead, giving himself up to the indescribable joy of making love with her, hoping it meant as much to her as it did to him, that what she might feel for him was strong enough to survive what he had to tell her tomorrow.

They finally fell asleep, bodies tangled together—only to be woken at dawn by the incessant ringing of the telephone.

Frowning, Seb struggled awake, reluctantly releasing Gina as he reached for the receiver.

'What is it?' he demanded in Italian. The shocking news imparted to him brought him to immediate alertness. *'Madre del Dio.'* He listened a moment longer, aware of Gina stirring beside him, then fired off some rapid questions. 'How many? What about supplies? Yes, of course. I will be there as soon as I can.'

Seb hung up the phone and flung back the duvet, reaching for his clothes. 'Gina. Wake up, *tesoro.'*

'What's happened?' she asked sleepily.

'There has been a building collapse at a tourist resort not far from here. There are many injured and missing. All medical help is needed, as well as blood donors, translators, and men to help dig. I have to go.'

'I'm coming with you.' Without hesitation, Gina was up and hurrying to dress.

'Put on layers,' he advised her.

'What about Nonna?'

Seb sat down to pull on his boots. 'I'll ring Evelina. She'll come to be with Maria.'

'Thank you.'

Already he was on the phone and making arrangements. By the time they were ready to leave, Evelina was hurrying up the drive, urging them to take care as they drove off with no idea what awaited them.

'Do you know what caused it?' Gina asked, and he was thankful for her calm.

'All I know is that this new development was built recently by a foreign company who brought in their own workers. There were rumours of corners being cut in the

construction, safety regulations not being complied with,'
Seb informed her, concentrating on negotiating the cliff
road as safely but as rapidly as possible. 'The storm yesterday and the sudden large amount of rain caused a
collapse of the unstable hillside ground and brought the
building down. There are still many tourists on Elba, and
this new complex of holiday apartments was nearly full.'

'How many people does the building hold?'

'Possibly two hundred. Maybe more.' It didn't bear
thinking about. 'Men, women and children.'

Minutes later they arrived on site, to a scene of devas-
tation. For a few seconds they both sat in silence as the
enormity of what lay before them sank in.

'Oh, Seb,' Gina breathed, her dismay obvious.

'I know.' He shook his head, trying to focus on what
needed to be done. 'For now we must do all we can to assist
those most in need, until more help arrives.'

Another more personal problem reared its ugly head,
and Seb swore aloud.

'What's wrong?' Gina asked, turning to him.

He took her hands in his. 'Before we become swallowed
up in this emergency, I need you to know that I care about
you—that I never meant it to happen like this,' he told her
urgently, the words rushing out in his need to try and limit
the damage.

'I don't understand.'

'I know, Gina. And that is my fault. It is *all* my fault.
And it is about me, not you, OK?' He glanced out of the
window and saw the policeman who had phoned him
hurrying in their direction. Desperate, he turned back to
Gina. 'I am sorry. When this is over I need to tell you
things about me—things I should have said ages ago and
was going to tell you today. Just remember how I feel
about you and what we are to each other. Please.'

'But—'

'Dottore Adriani—thank goodness you are on the

island. We need your expertise at once,' the policeman exclaimed, pulling open the driver's door.

Gina's eyes widened in shock. 'You're a doctor?'

Dio! He should have listened to Rico. And to Maria. If only he had swallowed his stupid pride and his fears, told Gina the truth from the beginning. But he had kept putting it off as it became more and more difficult. And now Gina had found out in the worst of ways.

'Later I will explain. I promise.' He cupped her face and gave her a quick, heated kiss, knowing this was not the time or the place. 'Come, Gina. I need you to be my hands. For now we have to help others.'

Withdrawing, she stared at him for a long moment as if she didn't know him at all, her eyes dark and wounded. 'All right,' she agreed, her voice cool and distant.

As she opened the passenger door and climbed out, Seb hurried after her. He had to focus on why they were here. The injured needed them, and that had to come before his own selfish concerns. But he didn't think he would ever forget that look on Gina's face—incomprehension, followed by disbelief, only to be replaced by hurt betrayal as realisation dawned. It drove a stake into his heart.

How was he ever going to make things right between them again?

CHAPTER EIGHT

CONFUSED and hurt, Gina battled to put her shock at the revelation about Seb aside and focus on what needed to be done. Her years of experience working in A and E, as well as being part of a trauma response team for major incidents such as serious accidents on the motorway, would stand her in good stead now. Even so, she surveyed the chaotic scene in front of her with bemusement.

It was almost impossible to believe that a modern four-storey building had stood here such a short time before. More than three-quarters of the curving structure cut into the hill had been brought down. The part of the end block still standing looked as if it had been sliced through by some giant axe, sheered away to reveal the remains of the rooms inside. Furniture balanced precariously on the edge. Clothes and possessions, dust and debris, were strewn everywhere. At least people in that section would have had the opportunity to get out. What chance would the holiday-makers in the rest of the now demolished building have had to escape, sleeping in their beds and unwitting of the disaster about to befall them?

A few survivors milled around in a daze, bleeding, bruised, concussed, crying…searching for missing loved ones. They were being comforted by a handful of early risers who had been away from the building, walking on

the beach or swimming before breakfast. Local men and
firefighters continued to arrive, working to clear and search
the vast expanse of rubble for trapped tourists, awaiting
specialist teams with heavy-lifting equipment, search dogs
and heat-seeking cameras.

Moments after she and Seb arrived on scene an advance
party of two more doctors and several nurses came from
the hospital in Portoferraio, over half an hour's drive away,
bringing much-needed supplies with them. Seb took
charge, his quiet authority unquestioned by anyone present
as he organised teams and assigned them tasks. He also ap-
pointed a dedicated triage officer, responsible for the clas-
sification of the injured. Following standard procedure for
incidents with a large number of casualties, patients would
be placed into one of four groups: life-threatening, urgent,
minor, and—sadly—dead and beyond help.

'I know what we face seems overwhelming, but we
must do the best we can with what we have,' he told them
in Italian, succinct and efficient. 'There are up to two
hundred people injured and trapped—this could go on all
day, even longer, as people are found and freed. More
emergency medical personnel are on the way, but the first
casualties need our help *now*. Watch for shock, crush
injuries and crush syndrome, internal bleeding, fractures
and head wounds. If you are unsure, or anything worries
you, ask for advice. Those casualties beyond hope we will
make as comfortable as possible, but we must concentrate
resources on those with the chance of survival. The most
severely injured will be taken by helicopter to the
mainland—we have to stabilise and evacuate them as
quickly and safely as possible. The walking wounded not
requiring immediate care should be watched by volunteers
until they can be dealt with. The police will record names,
nationalities and details of the missing. Any questions?'
There was silence. Seb nodded, his expression solemn.
'OK—let's get on.'

Everyone dispersed to their allotted tasks, and Gina found herself working alongside Seb. She still couldn't believe that he was a doctor, that he had never said a word despite all they had talked about. What else didn't she know about him? Could she trust anything he had said and done? Shaking her head, she forced away the painful questions and anxious doubts. People needed her, and she couldn't let them down. There would be time when this was over to get some answers.

'Are you all right, Gina?'

'Fine,' she murmured, unsure if his softly voiced question referred to what they now faced professionally or to the overwhelming shift in their personal situation.

She busied herself preparing instruments, drugs, oxygen, dressings and sundry supplies, so that everything they might need would be to hand. After they had both pulled on some hospital scrubs over their clothes, Gina took two pairs of gloves from the box and handed one to Seb.

'It's a while since I have done this kind of thing,' he told her as put them on, his vulnerability surprising her. 'Let us hope for the patients' sake that I am up to the task. And that my hands will hold out.'

In spite of her mental withdrawal from him, a wave of concern assailed her at his doubt over the decreased physical dexterity that so troubled him. Before she could reply, however, their first critically injured patient arrived—an unconscious man with a depressed skull fracture, broken shoulder and chest injuries.

It was the start of what seemed an unending stream, as more and more casualties were pulled alive from the rubble. As Seb had predicted, there was a predominance of crush injuries, fractures and deep-tissue wounds. Care had to be taken with crush syndrome, because prolonged pressure, when relieved, could cause shock, vascular problems, renal failure, even death. A doctor was on hand for each extraction, and difficult decisions had to be made—occasionally to sacrifice a limb to save a life.

Specialist search and medical teams soon arrived from the mainland, bringing further supplies and equipment. As the hours ticked by, she and Seb worked side by side on patient after patient, and she instinctively took on extra clinical tasks under his direction, to compensate for his reduced physical capacity.

Amongst the many people they treated from a variety of countries were a middle-aged woman with a severely fractured femur and extensive blood loss, two men with serious head injuries, a young woman with a dislocated shoulder, broken collarbone and two broken arms, a teenage boy with flail chest, a woman with extensive facial fractures and tissue damage, who had needed a cricothyroidotomy to re-establish her airway, and an older man with multiple lower leg fractures who was also complaining of chest pain which turned out to be cardiac.

They had all been stabilised and evacuated to hospital. And still the injured kept coming. Each case affected Gina, but it was the frightened, injured children who broke her heart.

Fighting weariness, she changed her gloves between patients and took a drink of the bottled water provided for them, allowing herself a glance at Seb. Over the years she had worked with many doctors, of varying abilities, and Seb was the very best of them. Despite the problem with his hands, his skill was extraordinary, and he was calm, compassionate and thorough. He had said he was rusty at this, so what kind of medicine did he normally do? Frowning, she noted the way he flexed his hands, grimacing with pain as he massaged his right wrist, thumb and forefinger. She loved him, but she was angry and confused, feeling betrayed, hurt, unsure. She needed time to think—but there was no chance of that at the moment.

Their next patient was a young man with chest injuries and breaks to the radius and ulna in his left arm, with the displaced bones piercing the skin. Confused and in pain, he was cold and pale, his skin clammy. While Seb carried out an initial assessment, Gina set to work inserting a cannula into the uninjured arm, and began running a crystalloid drip to replace fluids and ward off the effects of shock and blood loss.

'His breathing is distressed and he's tachycardic,' she told Seb, giving him details of blood pressure, respiration and pulse-rate.

'A couple of ribs are broken, and there are no breath sounds on the right side.' He paused a moment. 'There is tracheal deviation and he has distended neck veins.'

'Tension pneumothorax?'

'Yes.'

While Seb explained to the distressed young Italian what was happening, she busied herself preparing a local anaesthetic and the equipment he would require to aspirate the chest.

'Gina, I need your help.'

She looked up, trying to block out the regret and the plea for understanding in Seb's eyes. 'What is it?'

'I can't do this with my hands as they are,' he explained, his frustration evident.

She ached for his wounded pride and the loss of his full abilities. But with all the other medical teams as rushed as they were, there was no one else to call on. 'All right.' She moved around the makeshift treatment table to Seb's side.

'Have you ever done this before, Gina?'

'Once,' she admitted, remembering how terrified she had been, knowing there was no doctor on hand and that the woman in her care at the time would die if she didn't act fast. She'd later been commended for her actions, but it wasn't something she had ever wanted to do again. 'It was a long time ago.'

'I'm right here with you.' Seb's throaty reassurance rippled through her, and the inevitable but inappropriate awareness caught her off guard. 'We can do this... together.'

Gina sucked in a deep breath, trying to control both her nerves and her reaction to Seb. With the local anaesthetic having taken effect, she followed his detailed directions and inserted the needle into the second intercostal space in the midclavicular line, the aspirated air that escaped confirming his diagnosis. She was more scared than she wanted to admit as Seb talked her through the next step...making an incision in the fifth intercostal space, anterior to the mid-axillary line, and inserting a drain. He was with her every second, praising her, boosting her confidence, inserting a gloved finger into the incision to check the positioning, finally fitting the seal when the tube was correctly sited in the chest cavity. Relieved, her fingers shaking, Gina fixed it in place and checked the drain was working.

There was little time to think as they turned their attention to the badly fractured arm. After administering a top-up of analgesia through the intravenous access, she helped Seb straighten, dress and splint the damaged forearm, ensuring blood circulation, keeping the open wound sterile and applying support to the limb.

'Well done, *tesoro*, that was a great job. You were fantastic.' He smiled as their patient was taken to a helicopter for evacuation. 'We make a great team, no?'

A shaft of pain lanced through her and she turned away, hiding her emotional reaction as she cleared up and prepared for the next casualty. How could he act as if nothing had happened? As if lying to her didn't matter?

'Gina...'

'Not now,' she managed, knowing she would never get through the rest of this ordeal if she allowed thoughts of his deception to play on her mind.

They should have gone home hours ago, Seb acknowledged, but both he and Gina had needed to see it through for as long as they could be useful. It seemed impossible that anyone left buried under the rubble all these hours later could be alive and saved, but miraculously more *were* found, and they worked on to the point of exhaustion to give them the best care and the best chance possible.

The pain and seizing in his hands had increased, and now he could do less and less. His reduced ability made him impatient and angry, and confirmed that he would never be able to do surgery or trauma work again. Not on a regular basis. Thankfully he had kept up to date with emergency procedures, so he had been of some use at least, but as his hands had failed him, he had needed to rely more and more on Gina.

She had been incredible. A tower of strength. Calm, skilled, outwardly unfazed by anything thrown at her— although he could tell that some of the things they had dealt with had affected her, as they had him. She was totally professional and a terrific nurse, attuned to the patients' emotional need for reassurance while being efficient in attending to their clinical needs. They had worked so well together. It had restored some of his confidence, given him new hope for his future career. He *could* still be a doctor— *could* still make a difference and help people. It was a matter of finding a new niche. One which kept him true to himself this time. One which gave him the kind of self-respect that shone through in everything Gina did.

She had taught him so much about himself, had made him look with fresh eyes at his life, and she didn't even know it. He wanted so badly to share it with her, to explain his fears, his mistakes, to discuss where to go from here…but it could already be too late. He might have blown his best chance with the only woman to ever touch his heart, who had ever made him think of for ever. He could see and feel her doubts, her mistrust of him, and it pierced his soul.

It was early evening before they finally left the scene. Replacement medical teams from the mainland had relieved them, and search-and-rescue personnel were using heat-seeking cameras and a dog to locate the dozen people still missing and believed trapped in the lower layers of the collapsed building. The journey home was completed in a tense silence, and once back at the villa Gina walked inside and headed towards her own room in the guest wing.

'Gina, please. I—'

'I'm really tired, Seb.' She wouldn't meet his gaze, and fear clawed at his gut. 'I need to shower and sleep.'

'Of course. Thank you for all you did today. You were amazing.'

With a weary nod, she turned away. Reluctantly, Seb let her go, cursing himself for his stupidity. He had never meant to hurt her. And she *was* hurt. The pain in those big brown eyes broke his heart. Now he had no idea what to do to make things right—whether to go to her, or give her the space she asked for. How could he make her understand? Filled with uncertainty, he sent Evelina home, then checked on Maria before going to take a shower of his own, finally returning to the kitchen to force down a little of the food Evelina had left ready for them.

Some while later, exhausted and aching, he followed Gina's example and had an early night, lying in a bed that now seemed too big and empty. He was restless. Alone. He couldn't sleep without Gina in his arms. Succumbing to temptation, he got up and went to check on her—but she was not in her room. His anxiety increasing, he looked in on a sleeping Maria and found Gina curled up in the armchair beside the bed. Even in the dimness he could see the tracks of tears on her cheeks. Unable to bear her hurt or the separation between them a moment longer, he scooped her up in his arms and carried her back to his room.

'Seb…'

'Shh, *amore mia*,' he whispered at her soft, raw protest. 'Let me take care of you.' Tucking her into bed, he slid in beside her, gentling her, kissing her, licking away her tears. 'I'm sorry, Gina. So sorry.' Wrapping his arms around her, he kept her close. 'Please forgive me.'

He held her through the night, watching over her as she slept, but he was upset and concerned to wake up the next morning and find her gone from his bed. His alarm increasing, he hurried to dress and went in search of her. The villa was empty, but he found Maria and Evelina on the terrace. Evelina excused herself and bustled off to the kitchen to put on more coffee.

'Gina has gone for a walk,' Maria told him, understanding mixed with a hint of censure in her expression. 'She said she needed some time alone to think.'

Dannare! He didn't want Gina thinking…not until he had been able to talk to her, to explain, to tell her everything himself. That he had caused her hurt and had dented her trust in him was too painful to bear.

'Has she gone to the cove?' he asked Maria, his gaze straying down the cliffside to the crescent of beach far below.

'No, *caro*. She didn't say where she was going. And she didn't take her phone.'

Edgy and restless, he paced the terrace. He wanted to go after Gina. But how could he when he had no idea where she was?

'Sebastiano!'

Evelina's call had him turning towards the villa. 'Yes?'

'There is a call for you. They say it is important,' she informed him.

'Thank you.' Sighing, he faced Maria again. 'I am sorry. I should take this.'

'Of course. Try not to worry,' she added, patting his hand.

Seb knew her reassurance was well meant, but he couldn't help but worry. Concern for Gina and what this distance meant for them preyed on his mind as he headed indoors. The unexpected news he received only added to his tension.

'Is something the matter?' Maria asked as he returned to the terrace.

'That was the police in Florence. They have arrested the

man believed to be responsible for the knife attack in July,' he explained, sitting down to drink the coffee Evelina insisted he make time for. 'He was known to the police, but had gone into hiding after the incident. Yesterday he was picked up in Turin and returned to Florence. They want me there today to identify him, before he appears in court and is charged. It is the worst possible timing.'

'You must go, Sebastiano,' Evelina fretted.

'I know. There is a flight arranged for me. But I don't want to leave Gina. Especially now, with things unresolved between us.' He ran a hand through his hair in agitation. 'Where *is* she?'

Maria reached out and touched his arm. 'Perhaps Gina will return before it is time for you to leave for the airport.'

Seb could find little comfort in the words. More than anything he wished he could take Gina with him to Florence. But, even were she here to ask, he suspected she would decline—especially now, with the distance between them and so much unexplained. Besides, he knew she wouldn't leave Maria. He could only hope that time apart would help clarify things, that they could clear up their misunderstandings when he returned to Elba.

Going back indoors, he called for a progress report on yesterday's emergency. All casualties had been released from the rubble, and no one was missing, but the death toll had risen to fifteen. Still a miracle, he thought, given the enormity of what had happened. Next he phoned Rico and arranged for his cousin to meet his flight.

'It is good news that they have this man in custody at last,' Rico declared with satisfaction. 'Of course I will come for you, *cugino*. I will be happy to see you—you have been silent for days, and I am intrigued to hear all about the delectable Gina, who has obviously been keeping you very busy! Will she be with you?'

'Rico.' Seb growled the warning, in no mood for the teasing.

'What's wrong?'

'Nothing,' he lied. 'Not now, OK? I'll explain when I see you.'

He could tell Rico was worried, but thankfully his cousin didn't push the subject further on the phone. There would be enough of a lecture when Rico found out he had ignored his advice to confide in Gina straight away. Instead he had made a mess of everything, and he had no one to blame but himself.

Seb waited until the last minute, but Gina did not return to the house. Now he had to go, or he would be late for the private plane that awaited him at the island's small airport near La Pila, sited on the only flat land Elba had to offer, between Marina di Campo and Poggio. Filled with bitter disappointment, and an aching anxiety that things were falling apart, he said goodbye to Maria and Evelina and went out to the car.

But as he reached the bottom of the drive, he spied Gina walking along the road back towards the villa. Coming to a halt, he climbed out of the car.

'Gina!' The sad wariness in her dark eyes as she looked at him ripped out his heart. 'I did not want to go without seeing you.'

'You're leaving?' she asked, in surprise and confusion.

Cursing at the wobble in her voice, he took her in his arms, burying his face in her vanilla-scented hair. 'Only briefly. Maria will explain. The police have arrested a man for the knife attack. I have to go to Florence to identify him.'

'Of course.'

'We will talk when I come back, Gina. I hope that will be tonight, but it may be tomorrow. It depends on whether this is the man and if I have to attend court.' He cupped her face in his hands. 'I hurt you, and you cannot know how much I regret that. I am so sorry. I held back because of me, Gina, not you. Please give me the chance to explain when I return to Elba.'

Her nod was reluctant, and scarcely the promise he needed. Drawing her closer, he kissed her, putting everything into it, feeling the resistance drain out of her as she succumbed to the chemistry between them. He could only hope that their special connection would work in his favour.

With a monumental effort of will, he forced himself to release her and returned to the car. He drove away feeling deeply uneasy…and already terribly lonely without her.

The time passed with interminable slowness. Gina felt physically restless and emotionally unsettled, confused by all the doubts, worries and suspicions creating turmoil in her mind. Seb claimed he wanted to explain, but what excuse could there be for not telling her he was a doctor? Why had he deceived her?

She tried to occupy herself by devoting time to her grandmother, avoiding the subject of Seb and the pressing issue of returning home. They were due to travel the next day. The knowledge hung between them, unspoken. She couldn't bear the thought of leaving here, even with things the way they were, but Seb had not asked her to postpone her return to Scotland, and he had given no indication of his feelings—if he even had any. He had only claimed to want to set the record straight about why he had misled her. And then what would he do? Wave her goodbye?

Alone for the evening, the villa feeling empty without Seb's presence, she and her grandmother prepared and ate a simple pasta dish, and then settled down to watch television before bedtime. Gina had hoped there would be something interesting to distract her, but although her grandmother became absorbed in a documentary, Gina's own mind drifted. She was snapped from her reverie when the national Italian news came on, and she found herself staring at Seb's face on the screen. With a gasp, she sat up straight.

'Nonna?'

'I see him, *ragazza mia*.'

They watched in silence as the images unfolded, and Gina felt her blood chilling as she listened to a report of the knife attack and the arrest of the suspected assailant. The pictures showed Seb leaving the police station in Florence late that afternoon. He looked annoyed and frustrated at the intrusion of the journalists bombarding him with questions, at the press of microphones and cameras. The handsome man with him appeared equally irritated, bundling Seb through the crowd to where a sleek black Ferrari awaited.

Gina's mouth dropped open as the reality of what she was seeing and hearing sank in.

'Sebastiano Adriani, who dropped out of sight a few weeks ago and was believed to be convalescing overseas, returned to Florence today at the request of the police, to identify the man arrested for the assault in July. Dr Adriani went to the aid of the woman being attacked, and as a consequence suffered injuries to his hands that appear to have ended his high-flying career. The reconstructive plastic surgeon, renowned for his celebrity clients and equally famous girlfriends, was rumoured to have been dating young actress Lidia di Napoli at the time of the incident.

'Lidia di Napoli—seen here with her new beau, the recently divorced director of her current production—declined to answer questions. It is believed that the starlet abandoned her former boyfriend after his injuries threatened to bring an end to his celebrity status. But Dr Adriani has never been lacking female company.'

The words were accompanied by brief images of the stunning Lidia pouting at the camera, followed by library footage of Seb with a series of beautiful women on his arm. Then there was a short interview with the grateful victim of the knife incident, who praised Seb for his bravery and the way he had protected her. Gina wanted to shut out the pictures and the words, but she couldn't prevent herself from watching and listening as the report continued, breaking her heart in the process.

'*Questioned when leaving the police station today with his cousin, Riccardo Linardi, whose parents are wealthy corporate attorney Roberto Linardi and Sofia Linardi, known as a tireless charity campaigner, Dr Adriani refused to comment on where he has been, or discuss his career plans for the future. It is believed he will be staying overnight at the Linardi family's impressive Florentine mansion, rather than returning to his own luxury penthouse apartment in the city, which has remained unoccupied since July's incident.*

'*One report claims that Dr Adriani was seen on the island of Elba, giving medical aid to the casualties who survived yesterday's collapse of a block of tourist apartments that claimed fifteen lives. Neither hospital officials in Portoferraio nor the island's police will confirm or deny these rumours, and Dr Adriani's possible involvement, along with his whereabouts these last weeks, remain a mystery.*

'*Tomorrow Dr Adriani will appear in court, when the accused will face his first hearing. Bail is widely expected to be refused, given the accused's history of absconding.*'

Gina stared at the screen in disbelief. Not only was Seb a doctor, he was a wealthy and famous surgeon with an impressive list of celebrity clients. A renowned bachelor, he had a string of beautiful women at his disposal—women who were slim, sophisticated and polished...the complete opposite of herself. The Linardis, who owned this villa on Elba—the villa Seb had allowed her to believe he was caretaking—were actually his family, the aunt and uncle who had rescued him from the streets as a child. The Linardi family were rich, and part of Florentine society, with a lifestyle she couldn't even begin to imagine.

'Gina?' Her grandmother's voice held evident concern.

'He lied to me about *everything*!' She rose to her feet, switching off the television before pacing about the room. 'Not only about who and what he really is, but about the kind of world he comes from. He's Ferraris, Armani suits and champagne. I'm public transport, charity shop seconds and cheap Lambrusco!'

How he must have laughed at the naïve Scottish girl, taken in by an impossible fairytale. She felt hurt, angry and betrayed. And viciously self-critical of her own stupidity. She couldn't stay here. Couldn't face him again. She was so embarrassed. And so out of his league. He had his pick of beautiful women who fitted into his life as she never could. How could she have believed for a second that he could be attracted to and satisfied by her rounded curves, her lack of sophistication, her modest background? No wonder he hadn't wanted to let her into his world—not with the impossible chasm between them in terms of career and social status.

'Seb never cared about me, Nonna. He couldn't even be truthful.' She paused, battling emotion. 'We did what we came here to do. You are well enough for the journey. So we'll go home tomorrow, just as we planned.'

'But—'

'Please, Nonna. I can't stay here. Not now. I just *can't*.'

Ignoring her grandmother's protests, unable to hold back the tears, she retreated to her room, falling to the bed to cry out her hurt. Her foolish heart was shattered into tiny pieces. She had allowed herself to be caught up in an impossible dream, beguiled by Seb's charm, the magic of Elba and the romance of her grandparents' story. But there would be no happy ending for her as there had been fifty years ago for Maria and Matthew. Her brief re-awakening was over.

Her grandmother came quietly into the room. Sitting on the bed beside her, she gathered her into her arms, rocking her just as she had when she was a child.

'Oh, Nonna, I've been so stupid!' she sobbed.

'No, Gina, it is not your fault.' One hand stroked her hair as she soothed her. 'Seb should have told you sooner.'

Gina sniffed and wiped at her tears. 'Did you see the kind of women he dates all the time? He's not remotely interested in someone plain and ordinary like me.'

'You are not plain and ordinary,' her grandmother rebuked. 'My advice to you is to listen to what he has to say.'

'You're taking his side?' she accused.

'It is not a question of sides, *ragazza mia*. It is obvious you love him, and I don't think you should give up on something so right without fighting for it,' she cajoled, her hazel eyes wise and sad.

'But it's not right! I don't even know him. It's all been a lie from the beginning.' She took a tissue and blew her nose. 'It was a holiday fling—nothing more.'

Pain lanced inside her and she closed her eyes, trying to block out images of her days with Seb. He had never asked her to stay, had never told her he felt anything or asked if she did. From the first he had said she should experience the things Elba had to offer *while she was here*. Temporary. Short-term. She had done so. And now it was finished. She had fallen in love with a man she could never have beyond this unforgettable interlude.

Sucking in a ragged breath, she met her grandmother's anxious gaze. 'The fairytale is over, Nonna. It's time to return to real life.'

'What do you mean, they've gone?' Seb stared at Evelina in shocked disbelief, his heart threatening to stop entirely before resuming at a frantic beat. 'Gone where?'

'Home to Scotland.'

'When? Why?' he demanded, unable to get his head round the fact that Gina had left without waiting to hear what he needed to tell her.

Evelina looked both sad and accusing. 'This morning. I arrived after breakfast to find the taxi already here. Maria and I tried to persuade Gina to wait, but she was adamant…and distressed.'

'Distressed? Why? What happened?' The questions came in quick succession.

'You should have told her the truth when you had the

chance, Sebastiano.' Placing her hands on ample hips, she fixed him with a speaking glare. 'Gina saw the report about you on the television news last night…the pictures of you with all those fancy, insincere women. Including that actress Lidia—*il sfacciatella*. The hussy. It was a big shock to Gina to find out that way who and what you are.'

'*Dio!* No.' Shaken, Seb sat down and put his head in his hands.

He should have expected the media circus in Florence, but it had never crossed his mind that Gina might see him on TV—nor that the news would run some tabloid piece of gossip and innuendo that held scarcely a scrap of truth. Not that Gina would know that, because he'd never told her. All she knew was that he'd kept so much from her, and now she believed he had tricked her, made a fool of her, used her. And it wasn't true.

'Gina left you a note.' Evelina handed him a sealed envelope, shaking her head as she walked away, muttering to herself at his foolishness. '*Uomo stupido!*'

Evelina was right. He was a stupid man. He opened the envelope and a wave of fury washed over him when he found the money Gina had left to cover the cost of her and Maria's stay at the villa. Now he was mad! Then he read the note, her thanks for what he had done for her grandmother and for making it possible to succeed in what they had come to the island to do. The final sentences had him clenching his hands around the paper and swearing viciously at himself.

He should have told Gina all about himself from the beginning. But, as he had tried to explain to Rico, when his cousin had predictably read him the Riot Act last night, by the time he'd known she was genuine he'd been enjoying being accepted for the person he was, and not for his name or position or reputation.

'It's a lie, Seb. Albeit by omission,' Rico had protested. 'What are you afraid of—that she'll turn out to be a gold-digger like the rest of them?'

'Gina's the least materialistic person I've ever met,' he'd defended, thinking of her enjoyment of the most simple things. She was so refreshing, not to mention fun to be with, and he had never felt so relaxed and light-hearted with anyone as he did with her. 'But I thought it would change things. And I didn't want money or anything else to affect what we have. I'm a different person with her. I *like* me when I'm with her. And I wanted her to know the real me before the other stuff got in the way.'

'But she doesn't, does she? You've kept an important part of you back. Now she's found out by default that you're a doctor. It will be even worse if she discovers you've not been honest with her about the rest,' his cousin had warned, with what now turned out to be startling pre-sentiment. 'If she means something to you—'

'I love her, Rico.'

Saying the words out loud for the first time had cemented the truth in his mind. These last days with Gina had been the best of his life. The feelings were new to him, and he was scared but determined—and falling more and more in love with her by the hour. All other women seemed fake and uninteresting compared to her. He wanted Gina. She was the one. A few days, weeks or months with her would never be enough—he needed her in his life permanently.

Missing her like crazy, he had tried to phone last night from Florence, but her mobile had been switched off and there had been no reply from the house phone. It had been later than he had intended, because he had been delayed having dinner with Zio Roberto, Zia Sofia and Rico, so he had not worried unduly at being unable to speak with Gina. He had guessed that she and Maria were having an early night. It was only now he realised that she had seen the news and had been avoiding him.

He considered trying her mobile phone, but then thought better of it. He needed a proper strategy. If he rang or texted her now she would reject him. And it was all his fault. He had misjudged the situation from the first, and he had driven Gina away in the process, hurting her and destroying her trust in him. Unlike any other woman he had ever known, rather than seeing his money and his name as an advantage, to Gina it was a barrier, making a relationship between them impossible. He read again the final lines of the note crumpled in his hands...

> *I understand why you didn't tell me—I could never fit into your monied world or compete with the beautiful women you are used to. But I'll never forget my time with you on Elba. It was a lovely fairytale while it lasted. Now I have to face reality and go back to my own life. I wish you well with yours. Gina.*

Dio, she had it all wrong. He had never for a second imagined that she was not good enough for him. It was the other way round. *He* didn't deserve *her*. And no other woman held a candle to her. Somehow he had to make her understand. He'd been a fool, and now he risked losing the best thing that had ever happened to him because of it. His innocent subterfuge had backfired on him in a major way. It wasn't a mistake he would make again.

He was used to getting what he wanted. And he wanted Gina. No way was he giving up on her. She was the only woman he had ever loved, and it was time he fronted up and told her how he felt about her. Momentary doubt assailed him because he had no guarantee of her feelings for him. Yet if Gina didn't care, surely she wouldn't be so upset. The magic between them was special...the fairytale *was* real. He was the one who had messed up, so it was up to him to sort it out—to win back Gina's trust, to claim her heart and prove to her how much he loved her.

His mind made up, he reached for the telephone, ignoring the noisy banging of pots and pans from the kitchen as

Evelina made her displeasure at him known. Renewed determination fired inside him as his call was answered.

'Rico, it's me.' After updating his cousin on the latest events, he waited for the berating he deserved to come to an end, then, 'I need your help, *cugino*. Again. I have a plan.'

CHAPTER NINE

'THERE—that's the dressing done. We're all finished, Tam.' Gina pulled off her gloves, discarded the remains of the sterile wound pack, and smiled at the elderly man sitting on the treatment table. 'How does it feel now?'

'Much more comfortable, lass. I'm obliged to you.'

With painful dignity, over-long strands of straggly grey hair falling around his rugged face, the man leaned forward, pulled up his threadbare sock and rolled down the leg of his frayed trousers. Everyone in Strathlochan knew Old Tam. Of indeterminate age, he lived rough. He found it impossible to accept help from anyone, and got by doing odd jobs and living off scraps. His was a sad story of a lost job, lost home and lost family. He could be irritable, and he indulged in a drinking binge once or twice a year, but Gina knew he had a good heart. She wished he would accept the other things they could do for him, but he refused to go to hospital when poorly, rejected charity, and declined to take a place in a hostel, preferring the way of life he had become used to, suspicious of anyone who tried to interfere.

It was miracle enough that Tam had come to the centre to have the bad cut on his leg cleaned and treated. It had developed a nasty infection—not helped by the poor state of his living conditions. At least now they could keep the wound clean and dressed…and provide him with something hot to eat and drink. Given the way he had demolished a bowl of vegetable soup, a meat pie, a whole plateful of biscuits and two cups of tea, Tam clearly appreciated what the more informal and less pressured conditions of the new multi-purpose drop-in centre had to offer.

'Will you come back and see me in a few days?' Gina asked now, helping him to his feet and walking with him towards the front door, where his fiercely protective and constant companion Jock, a Jack Russell terrier, awaited him, barking noisily as he spied Tam returning.

'Aye, lass. Maybe I will.'

Gina knew it was as much of a promise as she could expect. Certain Tam would never take a course of tablets if she offered them, she had taken the precaution of giving him a broad spectrum antibiotic injection, along with a tetanus shot. She could only keep her fingers crossed he would return to have his dressing changed.

Smiling again, she held the door open for him. 'We're always here, Tam, so pop in any time that suits you.' Mentally crossing her fingers, she gave him a bag of fruit, and a couple of treats for Jock.

'Thank you, we'll enjoy these,' he allowed, and Gina let out a sigh of relief that he had not rejected the gift.

'Anything else I can do?'

He shook his head, untying the piece of bailer twine that served as Jock's lead, and bending to give the white and tan dog a gentle stroke. 'We'll be all right. You could tell Doc Gallagher that I'll take care of that gardening job for him.'

'I'll do that.' Bless Thorn for realising that Tam needed to feel useful, and to believe he was giving something in return. 'Take care.'

She watched him walk away, wondering where he went and how he managed. It made her ashamed of herself. She had so much to be thankful for, but all she had been able to think about this last week was the pain and desolation of losing Seb. Not that she had ever really had him. But leaving him and Elba had been heart-wrenching. A distraught Evelina had begged them to wait for Seb's return, but, aside from being unable to face him, Gina had felt awkward knowing the kindly woman had been party to his deception.

The taxi had dropped them at the hospital in Portoferraio, where Dottore Vasari had given her grandmother the official all-clear to travel. Then they had taken the ferry back to the mainland and caught the train to Pisa for their afternoon flight back to Scotland. Arriving home had brought mixed feelings...familiarity, warmth at her effusive welcome from Montgomery, but always the ceaseless ache of missing Seb and knowing that she would never see him again.

One day had passed into another, the nights dragging slowly as she found it hard to sleep without Seb, and when she did, his image filled her dreams. Everything made her think of him. Even starting her new job and catching up with her friends couldn't block the memories and her pain over Seb from her mind.

Trying to push the disturbing thoughts away, she went back inside the welcoming reception area, where Lesley Stuart claimed her attention. The centre's secretary turned her hand to anything that was needed, and had an uncanny knack of handling anyone from the fearful to the obstreperous with tact, compassion and firmness—a skill she claimed she had acquired raising three irrepressible boys alone. Gina had no idea where Thorn had found Lesley, but thank goodness he had, because everything ran like clockwork when she was around.

'Gina, Thorn asked if you could stop by his office before you leave,' the older woman informed her with a smile.

'Of course.' Gina tried to hide a flicker of anxiety as she wondered why the clinical director wanted to see her. 'Thanks, Lesley.'

After she had tidied the treatment room, written up

her notes and finished her final tasks of the day, she went to the staffroom to collect her things and say goodbye to a few of her colleagues who lingered there, sharing a chat over mugs of tea as they changed shift. A few moments later Gina stood outside Thorn's office and knocked on the door.

'Come in.'

Gina did as she was bid. Her boss was on the telephone, but he smiled and waved her to a chair, mouthing, "Won't be long," before returning his attention to the call. She sat down and waited, picking up from Thorn's end of the conversation that he was talking with Nic di Angelis, an Italian GP who worked locally. Thoughts of Italy inevitably brought images of Seb to mind. To prevent herself lingering on them, she tried to focus her attention on the man across the other side of the desk.

Thornton Gallagher was an enigma. There was an edge about him—something a bit dangerous and unconventional. He had not been in town long, but he was an excellent doctor, having proved himself during a six-month stint in Strathlochan's busy A and E department, which was where Gina had met him. In his early thirties, he was tall, with a rangy body and a leanly handsome face. He had unusual amber eyes and untamed, just-got-out-of-bed hair, its shade somewhere between dark blond and light brown.

Gina had always found Thorn good to work with, and he had been the perfect choice to run this centre. Experienced beyond his years in various areas of medicine, at home and abroad, he was full of exciting, often radical ideas for getting care delivered where and when it was needed. He was also not averse to bucking the system and going out on a limb for what he wanted.

As her boss said goodbye to Nic and hung up the phone, Gina found herself subjected to the full force of his enigmatic amber gaze.

'How have you found your first days here? Any

problems?' he asked, leaning his elbows on the desk and steepling his fingers under his chin.

'No, it's been good. I enjoy the work.' Despite her personal issues, she maintained her enthusiasm for her job, but Thorn's intense assessment made her uneasy. 'Why? Have I done something wrong?'

'Don't be silly, Gina.' He dismissed her question with an impatient wave of his hand. 'You're the best nurse I know. Why do you think I was determined to have you as part of my team?'

'Oh! Well, thank you,' she murmured, flattered and taken by surprise.

'How's Maria?'

Thorn's change of tack momentarily wrong-footed her. 'She's fine in herself. Our GP is keeping her on a maintenance dose of the diuretics, and monitoring her for any further fluid on the lungs and oedema...and investigating the cause.'

'It must have been a worry, her being taken ill while you were away?'

'Yes.' Pain lanced through her as she recalled Seb's arrival at Elba's hospital, his care and concern for her grandmother. 'Thankfully, all was well.'

Veiled amber eyes studied her, a pout of consideration shaping Thorn's mouth. 'And what about you?'

'What about me?'

'You've been pale and quiet,' he remarked, demonstrating once again that little escaped his notice. 'And sad since you came back from Italy.'

'I'm OK,' she lied, struggling to hold onto her composure.

She wasn't OK. She feared she never would be again. It was foolish, hopeless, but she loved Seb with every fragment of her broken heart, and she tormented herself over the way things had ended. Was her grandmother right? Had she made a mistake not waiting to see him? They were questions that plagued her in the darkest hours of the night. She had run because she had been hurt and scared. Scared she hadn't known him at all. Scared she could never be good enough for him. Scared Seb would explain why he had deceived her and then ask her to leave—tell her it had been fun, but... And it wasn't as if he had made any effort to contact her. Not that she expected him to. But a week's silence confirmed she had made the right decision. He was likely relieved to have it over without further awkwardness and embarrassment. But that didn't stop the welling of pain and disappointment.

'You met someone.' Thorn's uncanny insight spooked her. 'Your heart is still in Italy.'

Gina forced back an unwanted sting of tears. 'It wasn't to be.'

How could it be, when Seb was used to dating beautiful, rich women? She wouldn't fit in his world and they both knew it...that had to be why he had misled her and hidden the truth about himself from the beginning.

'You're in love with him.'

'Yes,' she found herself admitting. She huffed out a breath, wishing Thorn wasn't so adept at zeroing in on people's emotions and getting them to confide in him, even when they didn't mean to. 'But there's nothing I can do about it.'

Thorn remained silent, continuing to watch her, his expression unreadable, a small, mysterious smile pulling at his mouth.

'Anyway, you asked about work. I've just seen Old Tam,' she said, determined to divert the conversation away from herself. 'Whether he comes back to have his wound re-dressed remains to be seen. He asked me to tell you he'll take care of the job you asked him to do.'

Knowing amusement sparked in Thorn's amber eyes. 'Thanks. Are you off home now?'

'Yes.' Thankful to be let off the hook—because he had most surely sussed out her ploy—she rose to her feet.

'After a stop at the supermarket on the way back. Holly and Ruth are coming round later.'

'I'll walk you out.'

Puzzled, because it wasn't a normal thing for him to do, she watched as he gracefully eased his athletic frame from the chair and walked across to open the door. She might not be attracted herself, but she could understand why many other women were. It wasn't just Thorn's looks, it was the bad-boy edge he had about him.

'Thanks. But you don't have to bother. You're busy,' she added, not wanting to be impolite.

'I'm about to show someone around the centre. He's interested in making a donation…of both money and expertise. A skilled doctor, he could be on board full-time.' He paused, his unfathomable gaze watchful. 'Let's hope we can satisfy his needs and give him all he wants to stay in Strathlochan.'

'The additional help would be welcome,' Gina agreed, thinking of the benefit to the centre of having an extra full-time doctor on staff with Thorn, rather than relying so much on the voluntary efforts of local GPs and hospital staff. 'Is there anything I can do to help?'

Thorn's mysterious smile widened as they stepped out of the building and into the small car park. 'Later, no doubt. But I have this end covered for now.'

'OK.' She fastened the zip of her jacket against the kiss of the cool autumn air, hooking the strap of her bag over her shoulder. 'I hope it works out.'

'Me, too.'

She frowned at the amused edge to his tone, sensing there was something he wasn't telling her. 'Goodnight, Thorn.'

''Night,' he answered. 'Give my love to Maria.'

'I will.' She was about to step away when Thorn tugged gently on the long braid hanging down her back. Halting, she turned and faced him again. 'Yes?'

For a long moment his gaze searched hers. Then he

nodded and smiled again. 'You never know what waits for you around the next corner. Good luck, Gina.'

More confused than ever by Thorn's curious comments, she walked away, feeling his gaze on her until she turned out on to the street. Shaking her head, she switched on her mobile phone, finding two texts awaiting her—both Holly and Ruth cancelling their evening. Disappointed, she rang her grandmother to ask if she needed anything from the shops, and to let her know she was on her way home.

Home. She loved it here, but she had felt so restless since returning from Italy. Her time on Elba with Seb had been a fantasy. Now she was back to earth with a bump, with only the memories of a few snatched days and nights of happiness to sustain her...memories of a magical passion she knew she would never experience again.

Seb watched from his hire car as Gina left the building, his breath catching and his heart kicking as he drank in his first glimpse of her for far too many days. Then his eyes narrowed as he noted the man who followed her out. From where Seb was sitting, the guy was being far too familiar with Gina—a fact borne out when she turned to walk away and the man reached out a hand to catch her braid.

'Who the hell is he?' Seb growled, overcome by a wave of possessive jealousy.

Nic di Angelis, his companion in the car, chuckled. 'No one for you to worry about, *mio amico*. That's Thorn.'

'Thornton Gallagher?' he exclaimed, unable to hide his shock.

'The one and only.'

As Gina disappeared from view, Seb returned his attention to Thorn, watching as he sauntered in their direction. He had spoken to the clinic's director several times by phone in the last days, and he had formed an image in his mind of an older man—a no-nonsense and deeply committed doctor. Yet Thorn was around his own age. Needing to be open about the reasons for his interest in the centre, and where Gina fitted into his plans, Seb had uncharacteristically taken Thorn into his confidence, finding a willing ally.

Even with Rico, Thorn and Nic pulling strings for him it had taken several days to get his papers in order and make the necessary arrangements for major changes in his life—the success of which rested on seeking Gina's forgiveness. He didn't know what he would do if he couldn't talk her round, if she didn't love him even a fraction as much as he loved her.

Nic and his lovely wife Hannah had welcomed him to their home the previous night, after his arrival from Italy, offering him a place to stay. They had been friendly and helpful, and Nic had also shared his experiences of living and working as a doctor in rural Scotland.

'I've been here nearly five years to the day, and they have been the happiest of my life,' he had told him with obvious sincerity. 'It's a great place to live.'

'What about the weather? The cold winters?'

'It's not that bad. And there is much to be said for cuddling up in front of a log fire with the woman you love,' Nic had responded, warm amusement in his dark eyes.

'I would be happy anywhere with Gina by my side,' he'd agreed, filled with renewed determination. 'Now I have to make it happen.'

Earlier that day he had visited Maria and won her support. She had invited Gina's friends Holly and Ruth for lunch and, after their initial reticence, he had been able to bring them on board, too. All that remained now was to meet Thorn in person, look round the centre…and then face Gina.

'I can see why you told me to dress casually,' he commented as Thorn, wearing jeans and a sweatshirt bearing the centre's logo, approached the car.

'Thorn doesn't stand on ceremony. But don't be fooled by his relaxed, lazy air…he's as sharp as they come,' his new friend advised. 'He's a first-class doctor, and his maverick nature makes him perfect for this job.'

As Nic opened the passenger door and climbed out, Seb followed suit, slipping from behind the steering wheel and exchanging a firm handshake with the man he hoped to be working with in the very near future.

'Good to meet you, Seb.' Thorn smiled as Nic introduced them. 'The coast is clear. Gina's heading home via the supermarket, so you have a while.'

'She doesn't know I'm here?'

'She has no idea,' Thorn confirmed. 'But I wanted to test the waters. Even I can be subtle when needed.' A wry smile curved his mouth before he sobered. 'If I didn't think this was in her best interests, we wouldn't be here. Come on in and have a look around.'

Gina pushed open the front door, juggling keys and carrier bags as she was greeted by an enthusiastic Monty, his wagging tail beating a tattoo against the hall radiator. 'Let me put the shopping down first.'

The dog trotted after her to the kitchen, where she found her grandmother putting the finishing touches to an evening meal. Surprised at this change to their normal routine, Gina halted and stared at her.

'Gina!' The older woman smiled. 'Good—you are home.'

'Is everything all right?' she queried, setting her bags down on a free piece of worktop.

'Yes, of course. As Holly and Ruth are not coming, I wanted to make you something special for supper,' she informed her, turning back to the counter. 'I have done your favourite apple and blackberry crumble for pudding!'

'Nonna, it's kind of you, but I'm really not that hungry.'

'Nonsense. You must start eating properly again,' her grandmother chided.

Sighing, Gina put the shopping away. 'How did you know Holly and Ruth had cancelled?'

'I talked to Ruth earlier.' Her grandmother's cheeks were stained pink, and Gina's gaze sharpened in suspicion. 'She was telling me the latest news about that Julia—Holly's awful sister. Holly's so upset. How Gus Buchanan—'

'Nonna,' Gina interrupted, confused and frustrated.

'I just wanted to do something nice for you,' her grandmother explained, making her feel bad for her lack of appreciation. 'I know you are tired. And sad.'

Gina closed her eyes, trying to shut out the pain. 'I'm fine.'

'We both know that isn't true...and why.' Shaking her head, her grandmother tutted again. 'Go upstairs, now. Have a shower and change into a nice frock.'

'But...'

'Make the effort for me, *ragazza mia*,' she requested firmly. 'Please?'

Anxious to escape another discussion about Seb, and their disagreement over leaving Elba so suddenly, Gina escaped the kitchen and went upstairs to change. It was unlike her grandmother to be so dogged, or so tactless—yet she gave her no peace, seeming unable to understand why she was so hurt by Seb's lies. Her heart aching, she sat on her bed, feeling listless and very much alone.

She missed Seb so much. How could she have fallen in love with him in such a short time? She would never feel again as she had with him. Not just the spectacular experience of making love with him, but everything...just being with him, how he made her feel, the way he listened to her. Yet he had shared so little about himself.

Her gaze strayed to the bedside chest. Apart from memories and a broken heart, she had taken only three things from Elba. The beautiful piece of Elbaite Seb had bought her, with its delicate colours and intriguing textures. The white rose, pressed now between the pages of a book. And she had kept his jumper—the one he had taken off and pulled over her head that night on the terrace. She had never given it back. Now she tortured herself, sleeping in it, keeping it, a small part of Seb, close to her. She picked it up now and buried her face in it, breathing in his lingering scent.

'Gina! I can't hear the water running!'

As her grandmother called impatiently up the stairs, Gina choked back a fresh welling of tears. Setting the jumper aside, she rose to her feet, taking off her trousers and the sweatshirt with the centre's logo that constituted their informal uniform. After a quick shower, she stared at her wardrobe. Her red dress caught her eye and new pain lanced inside her. She couldn't wear it—not without re-membering her night out with Seb at the restaurant in Marciana Marina…the night he had kissed her for the first time. That sensuous, confident woman had been put back under wraps again. There was no room for her here—and no Seb to set her free.

Drawing in an unsteady breath, she pulled out a floaty skirt and a button-through top, her fingers shaking as she dressed. Her grandmother was behaving very oddly. Gina just hoped she was not to be subjected to another lecture about Seb, or she would never survive the evening with her emotions intact.

'What do you think?' Thorn asked, closing his office door and bringing their tour of the centre to an end.

Seb had met the staff on duty, and found the place and the whole philosophy behind it exciting and intriguing. 'I'm really impressed. And enthusiastic.'

'You are vastly over-qualified, but if you are sure this is what you want, I'd be delighted to have someone of your experience on the team here.'

'Thank you. I might be unable to perform surgery again, but Gina helped show me that I can still be useful—still be needed,' he told Thorn, having already confided in him about his background as a child on the streets. 'I'll need to brush up on some areas, and I will be happy to take any courses you recommend. I've heard so much about this place from Gina, and I share her belief in what you are doing.'

Thorn nodded, his amber gaze assessing. 'And now you need to see her.'

'Yes.' Anxiety rippled through him at what still lay ahead. 'The final decision on whether I stay or go rests with her.'

'I wish you luck.' Thorn shook his hand, his expression serious. 'As a friend to Gina—and I hope soon to you— get this right, Seb. You hurt her once. Don't do it again.'

Admiring the man, and appreciating his genuine concern, Seb nodded and went outside to join Nic. Hannah had arrived to collect her husband, and they wished him well on the next stage of his venture. He watched them leave before crossing to his hire car and making the short drive back to Gina and Maria's cottage.

He planned to win Gina back—to prove to her that he was worthy of her and not some flash surgeon who had lost his soul and forgotten why he had become a doctor. Having Gina in his life had opened his eyes and his heart to where he had been going wrong. It wasn't too late to get his career back on track. He just hoped it wasn't too late for him and Gina.

As agreed with Maria, he used the key she had given him and slipped in through the back door of the small but homely cottage situated in a quiet, leafy road. The views of the hills and woods appealed to him—he loved what he had seen of the region in his first hours here, and he couldn't wait to explore with Gina. He hunkered down in the kitchen to greet Monty, having bonded with the dog earlier in the day. Maria cracked the door open and peeped round it.

'Gina will be down any moment,' she whispered, hazel eyes sparkling with conspiratorial delight. 'I'll lure her into the living room. You come along when you are ready.'

Seb nodded. The door closed again, and his heart lurched as he heard Gina's footfall on the stairs and Maria's voice calling to her. He'd give them a few moments—and himself time to try and steady his nerves. He was more scared than at any time in his life. He had support from

Maria, Rico, Thorn, Nic and Hannah, even Ruth and Holly. Now it was all down to him. Could he persuade Gina to forgive him and grant him a second chance? He *had* to succeed. Life without Gina was unthinkable, unbearable.

Leaving a disgruntled Monty in the kitchen, and closing the door behind him, he walked quietly along the corridor. Any moment now he would face the most important test of his life. Female voices became clearer, and Gina's words temporarily shocked him to immobility...

Gina stood in the living room, her hands tightly clasping the back of a chair as she faced her grandmother's latest challenge.

'Have you given any more thought to what I said about Seb?' Hazel eyes reflected fierce determination. 'It's been a week, Gina.'

She knew how long it had been—was aware of every painful second. 'Seb lied to me, Nonna.'

'Did he tell you he was caretaker of the villa?'

'No. But he knew that was what I thought, and he did nothing to correct me. He never told me he was a surgeon, that he was rich and famous, or that his family owned the place. He deliberately deceived me.'

'And why do you think he would do that?'

Gina shrugged, upset that her grandmother was pushing her like this. 'We've been through all this before, and it isn't going to change anything. It was stupid of me to ever believe in a fantasy,' she stated, hurting inside at the thought of Seb's duplicity and her own foolishness.

'You don't think there may be other, more understandable reasons, *ragazza mia*?'

'What reasons could there be?' Her hands tightened their grip on the chair as she battled her emotions. 'Seb didn't respect or care about me enough to be truthful, to trust me. And I'm nothing compared to the women he's used to dating.

Her grandmother tutted in annoyance. 'That's rubbish.'

'Anyway, it was different when I thought Seb was just a normal guy. I—'

'Exactly.'

With a cry of shock, Gina spun round as Seb's voice sounded behind her. Her heart thudded wildly at the sight of him. He looked divine...casually rumpled, the thickness of his hair tossed by the early autumn breeze, the beginnings of a five o'clock shadow darkening his jawline, that delectable body encased in dark-grey chinos and a chunky black jumper. For a moment she swayed, certain she must be hallucinating. But when she closed her eyes and opened them again Seb was still there. She glanced accusingly at her grandmother, whose expression was one of defiance mixed with guilt.

'Do not blame Maria,' Seb intervened. 'I am the one who needs to explain things to you. I was desperate enough to follow you here as soon as I could arrange it, and to appeal to your grandmother and your friends for their help.'

'Why?' she whispered.

'Will you listen to what I have to say?' Warm caramel-coloured eyes she had never expected to see again looked deeply into hers. 'Please, Gina?'

Racked with indecision, Gina hesitated. She was aware of her grandmother exiting the room, but when Seb tried to close the distance between them she backed up, keeping out of his reach. If he touched her now, all her defences and common sense would crumble. The front doorbell rang, startling her, and her eyes widened as her grandmother opened it and both Holly and Ruth stepped into the hall, conspiratorial smiles on their faces. Holly gave her a thumbs-up.

'What's going on?' Gina demanded.

'I'm staying the night with Ruth.' Smiling, her grandmother picked up a small overnight bag. 'You and Seb need to be alone. Supper is ready in the kitchen—it will keep until you want it.'

Gina's mouth dropped open. She couldn't believe any of this. But before she could find her voice to protest, the girls had ushered her grandmother outside. The front door closed. She was, indeed, alone with Seb.

'What's going on? Why are you here?' Her hands were shaking badly, so she clasped them tightly together. Unable to help herself, she let her gaze drink in the sight of him, but the pain inside her couldn't be denied. Pent-up tears stung her eyes. 'You lied to me from the beginning. I wasn't good enough for you.'

'No!' Gina's accusations cut through him, and seeing the mistrust and tears bruising her dark eyes made him realise just how deeply he had hurt her, how badly he had misjudged everything. 'It was never that, Gina. It was *me*, not you.'

'I don't understand.'

He cursed the wobble in her voice, desperately needing to hold her, but knowing he had to give her space until he had explained. 'I know, *amore mia*, and that is my fault. I was ashamed. I so admired your passion, your goodness, your principles. I feared that when you found out how shallow my life and career had become you would be dis-appointed in me, reject me.'

For long moments she stared at him in silence, and he waited, hiding nothing from her. 'You're serious,' she whispered, confusion, disbelief and wonder all layered through her voice.

'I am. Will you allow me to explain from the begin-ning?' He held his breath, knowing how important her answer was, uncaring that he was begging. 'Please, Gina.'

She bit her lip, and desire flared inside him. He couldn't wait to taste her mouth again, to taste her all over, hold her, make love with her. Finally, when he thought he couldn't stand the wait another second, she nodded—although she remained too far away, regarding him with suspicion. Not that he could blame her. He had this one chance…he couldn't blow it.

Leaving nothing out, he told her all about Antonella, about the people who'd used him, the way he had been encouraged to change the direction of his career. He talked of the Linardis, even of how he had operated free of charge on Paolo's young daughter when she had been badly injured in an accident on Elba, and how he'd only felt fulfilled doing the *pro bono* work.

'I was attracted to you the second I saw you,' he continued, searching her face, hoping she understood and believed him. 'But I was wary—suspicious of your presence because of past press intrusion. At first I thought there was a possibility you were a journalist, looking for a clever way in…that's why I was cagey and didn't tell you who I was.' Her mouth opened in protest and he rushed on before she could interrupt. 'As soon as I got to know you it was clear you were totally genuine. By then my feelings for you were escalating and I was overwhelmed by how natural you were. I'd never met anyone like you, Gina. You treated me as a normal person. I liked it—liked that you saw *me*. The intention was never to trick you or deceive you—I just wanted some time, so you would know the real me, in the hope that the other things would no longer matter when you knew.'

'Seb…'

Scared in case she stopped listening, he held up a hand. 'Wait—please. I need to tell you it all, to explain what you did for me.'

'What *I* did for *you*?' she repeated, a stunned expression in her eyes.

'Yes—in so many ways.' To resist the temptation of reaching for her, he sat on the edge of the sofa, his elbows resting on his knees. 'You've taught me so much about myself, Gina.'

Sitting opposite, she looked at him in confusion. 'How?'

'I've never told anyone else the things I told you about my past. Not even my cousin Rico. Talking to you, listening to you, I realised how much I have been unconsciously striving to prove myself worthy of the faith and love the Linardis showed me when they took me in. I never felt good enough—I needed to belong. I had some success in my surgical career, then I was guided down a road I should never have agreed to travel. But I did. And that responsibility rests with me,' he admitted, making no excuses. 'As I became known, all people saw was what I could do for them—and the money and the fame. You are the first person to see who I am on the inside, without all the trappings. You made me like myself. And hearing you speak of your work with such passion and dedication showed me how far I had come from my roots. I had forgotten why I had become a doctor in the first place.

'I feared you would hate what I did—would judge me for having wasted my surgical skills—' He broke off and looked at his hands. 'Having these injuries may have been a blessing in disguise. Without them I would never have gone to Elba and I would never have met you. Learning about your values, your down-to-earth goodness, made me reassess my life and find it wanting. I had taken that wrong turning for the wrong reasons. Now I want to believe in something again, to use my medical knowledge to do good. I don't care about the money. I never have. And I hate being recognised. Those things are not important. I want a second chance with my work—but most important of all I want you.

'In such a short time you have opened my eyes to what was wrong with my life. I was at a turning point, coming to terms with losing surgery. I didn't know who I was or what I wanted to be. For years I have been used for my name and my position. But for you, Gina, I was just Seb. I was myself with you. I know I should have told you everything from the first, but I was already in so deep and I cared so much that it became harder and harder to find the right moment. I was frightened it would change things between us—change how you saw me.' A wry, self-depre-cating laugh escaped. 'I was right, no? It did make a dif-ference. It opened that gulf and spoiled everything. You no longer saw *me*.'

Seb looked up, and the sincerity tinged with fearful doubt in his eyes brought a lump to Gina's throat.

Yes, he should have told her about himself. But she had some understanding now of why he hadn't. She was also uncomfortably aware that he was right...at least in part. She *had* reacted to the news by forgetting all she knew him to be. Her attitude towards him *had* changed. She had seen only the differences between them, believing there to be an unbridgeable chasm. Would her reaction have been more measured had he told her when they had first met? She wasn't sure, but she feared that had she known at the start that Seb was a rich and famous surgeon she would have withdrawn, put up barriers, never become involved with him despite their attraction and sexual chemistry. She would have judged him—not harshly for the work he did, but believing she wasn't good enough for him.

'Seb...' She paused, struggling for the right words. 'I was frightened by the truth. Scared of everything I imagined came with you,' she admitted, knowing she had to be equally honest. 'But I would never have judged you about your work. And money means nothing to me.'

'No, but it came between us just the same. Instead of seeing what it would do for you, as others have done, you saw it as an obstacle, and it changed the way you saw me—us. You mistakenly decided that we couldn't fit. But we can—we *do*.'

'What about all those women? They are beautiful, thin, sophisticated—'

Again he interrupted her, edging closer, his fingers on

her lips silencing her protests and sending shivers of sensation zinging through her body. 'Gina, the truth is that I have *never* taken a women to my home, in Florence or in Elba, until you. The women I was seen out with were all using me to further their names and careers. They liked to be seen on my arm, to meet people who could help them, and I had convenient escorts to official functions. I wasn't "dating" them, I had no relationship with any of them, and there was no romance, no emotion—and ninety-nine times out of a hundred no sex. My career was everything to me. I wasn't interested in a relationship...until I met you.'

'But—'

'But nothing,' he chided softly, cupping her face in his hands. 'Those women are vain, artificial and uncaring, interested only in themselves. I am not attracted to any of them. You are so much more beautiful in every way, Gina. You are real and honest and generous, the most natural, giving person I've ever known.' The pad of one thumb brushed across her trembling lips and she couldn't look away from the raw expression in his eyes. 'You are the only woman who has ever stolen my heart, who I have ever needed, who I want to spend the rest of my life with. I've missed you so much. I love you, Gina. I don't want to live another day without you by my side, or another night without you in my arms.'

Tears escaped, squeezing between her lashes and trickling down her cheeks. Seb was a proud man, independent, unused to needing or trusting anyone, and yet here he was, vulnerable and open, laying his heart on the line—for her. There was much to talk about, and to understand, but she knew she wanted to face whatever life threw at her with him. She loved him beyond bearing. Stifling a sob, she melted into his embrace.

A shuddering breath of relief rushed out of him as he wrapped his arms around her and held her tight. She absorbed his strength, breathed in his familiar scent, knowing she was truly home...at last.

'We'll work everything out, *amore mia*.' His voice was shaky, his breath warm against her skin as he whispered in her ear. 'I love you more than life itself. Never leave me again. Promise me.'

'I promise. I love you, too.'

He pulled back a few inches and for endless moments their gazes locked, silent messages and reassurances exchanged. Then he was kissing her with all the devastating skill and desire she had come to know so well and had missed so terribly these last lonely days. She took everything and gave it back with enthusiasm, swept along in a whirlwind of passion and love. Until, that was, they were interrupted by Monty, who pushed his way between them. Laughing, they tried to hold off the exuberant dog.

'I come as a package, Seb,' she reminded him, seriousness underlying the humour. 'Not just Monty, but Nonna, too.'

'I know that, *amata*. And I wouldn't have it any other way. Monty and I are already good friends, and Maria is very special to me,' he reassured her, one warm palm cupping her cheek. 'Her place will be with us—always.'

Closing her eyes, she rubbed her face against him, revelling in his touch. 'So what do you plan to do...for the future, I mean?'

'I've been making arrangements with Thorn. Today I looked round your wonderful centre,' he admitted, laughing at her gasp of shock.

'It was *you*!' That was why her boss had been behaving oddly, asking her those questions. 'Thorn knew all along!'

'He did. My cousin Rico and Nic di Angelis have also been helping me.'

Startled, she pulled back and looked at him. 'How do you know Nic?'

'I didn't...not until recently.' He smiled and ran the fingers of one hand through her hair. 'The name Strathlochan struck a chord when you mentioned it, but I couldn't remember why. Rico reminded me. He worked with Nic for a time in Milan, and they have remained good friends. Rico came over here for his wedding. He put me in touch with Nic.'

'I see,' she murmured, feeling dazed.

'Everything is in order for me to come here. I want us to be together, Gina, and I'll be happy anywhere you are. We can live here in Strathlochan and have holidays on Elba. If you will have me, we can work side by side during the day...and love each other every night.'

It was a shock to realise how much organising and manoeuvring had gone on behind her back. Her grandmother, Holly, Ruth, Thorn, even Nic and Hannah, she discovered, had all joined forces to help Seb plan all this. She might have been disgruntled if she hadn't been so blissfully happy that Seb was here, that he loved her, wanted her, had followed her to Strathlochan. She loved the idea of working with him at the drop-in centre—loved even more his plans for their nights together.

'What about your family?' Doubts and insecurities assailed her. 'Maybe they won't approve of me.'

'Rico has demanded to meet you from the first day,' he told her, shocking her anew. 'He's been your champion, telling me I am an idiot for keeping things from you. He wanted to come straight over to Elba to see you and Maria, but I wouldn't let him.'

'Why not?' she queried, concerned despite his arguments to the contrary that he had been ashamed of her.

'Because Rico is charming and handsome and outgoing. I didn't want to risk you falling for him instead of me.'

The admission, so obviously sincere, revealing his vulnerability, stunned her. 'You shouldn't have worried. I would never have seen anyone but you...not from the instant I met you on the beach,' she vowed, laying her own hand against his stubbled jaw, seeing his eyes heat and darken.

He gave her a hasty but delicious kiss before drawing back. 'As for Zio Roberto and Zia Sofia—they are equally enthusiastic,' he reassured her. 'They are eager to meet you. Eager, too, to meet Maria and hear her memories of Elba. They are fully supportive of what you came to the beach to do. Zio Roberto built the villa as a fifth anniversary present for Zia Sofia thirty years ago. It is a special place for all our combined family.'

'It is.'

The familiar burn of heated desire flaring inside her, she met his gaze, her fingertips exploring, relearning the contours of his face. He caught her hand, his lips and tongue teasing her palm, causing the ache of need to knot deep within her.

With Monty curling up in front of the fire, Seb drew her down with him on the sofa. 'I love you. You are my life,' he murmured huskily, moments before his mouth met hers. '*Per sempre*, Gina *mia*…for ever.'

Fresh tears, joyful tears, stung Gina's eyes. Just a short while ago she had been in despair. Now she was the happiest woman alive. How could she be this lucky? Wrapping her arms around him, wriggling on top of him, she showed Seb in every way how much she loved him.

History had repeated itself after all, and Elba had worked her magic a second time. The fates had smiled on them as they had on Maria and Matthew, leading them to meet and fall in love in the same special place half a century later. Gina smiled and gave thanks. Like her grandparents before them, she and Seb had found togetherness, a secure bond, and a love to last a lifetime. They were blessed indeed.

1209 Gen Std HB

MILLS & BOON

ROMANCE

Untamed Billionaire, Undressed Virgin	Anna Cleary
Pleasure, Pregnancy and a Proposition	Heidi Rice
Exposed: Misbehaving with the Magnate	Kelly Hunter
Pregnant by the Playboy Tycoon	Anne Oliver
The Secret Mistress Arrangement	Kimberly Lang
The Marcolini Blackmail Marriage	Melanie Milburne
Bought: One Night, One Marriage	Natalie Anderson
Confessions of a Millionaire's Mistress	Robyn Grady
Housekeeper at His Beck and Call	Susan Stephens
Public Scandal, Private Mistress	Susan Napier
Surrender to the Playboy Sheikh	Kate Hardy
The Magnate's Indecent Proposal	Ally Blake
His Mistress, His Terms	Trish Wylie
The Boss's Bedroom Agenda	Nicola Marsh
Master of Mallarinka & Hired: His Personal Assistant	Way & Steele
The Lucchesi Bride & Adopted: One Baby	Winters & Oakley
An Italian Affair	Margaret McDonagh
Small Miracles	Jennifer Taylor

HISTORICAL

One Unashamed Night	Sophia James
The Captain's Mysterious Lady	Mary Nichols
The Major and the Pickpocket	Lucy Ashford

MEDICAL™

A Winter Bride	Meredith Webber
A Dedicated Lady	Gill Sanderson
An Unexpected Choice	Alison Roberts
Nice And Easy	Josie Metcalfe

1209 Gen Std LP

MILLS & BOON

JANUARY 2010 LARGE PRINT TITLES

ROMANCE

Marchese's Forgotten Bride	Michelle Reid
The Brazilian Millionaire's Love-Child	Anne Mather
Powerful Greek, Unworldly Wife	Sarah Morgan
The Virgin Secretary's Impossible Boss	Carole Mortimer
Claimed: Secret Royal Son	Marion Lennox
Expecting Miracle Twins	Barbara Hannay
A Trip with the Tycoon	Nicola Marsh
Invitation to the Boss's Ball	Fiona Harper

HISTORICAL

The Piratical Miss Ravenhurst	Louise Allen
His Forbidden Liaison	Joanna Maitland
An Innocent Debutante in Hanover Square	Anne Herries

MEDICAL™

The Valtieri Marriage Deal	Caroline Anderson
The Rebel and the Baby Doctor	Joanna Neil
The Country Doctor's Daughter	Gill Sanderson
Surgeon Boss, Bachelor Dad	Lucy Clark
The Greek Doctor's Proposal	Molly Evans
Single Father: Wife and Mother Wanted	Sharon Archer

MILLS & BOON

FEBRUARY 2010 HARDBACK TITLES

ROMANCE

At the Boss's Beck and Call	Anna Cleary
Hot-Shot Tycoon, Indecent Proposal	Heidi Rice
Revealed: A Prince and A Pregnancy	Kelly Hunter
Hot Boss, Wicked Nights	Anne Oliver
The Millionaire's Misbehaving Mistress	Kimberly Lang
Between the Italian's Sheets	Natalie Anderson
Naughty Nights in the Millionaire's Mansion	Robyn Grady
Sheikh Boss, Hot Desert Nights	Susan Stephens
Bought: One Damsel in Distress	Lucy King
The Billionaire's Bought Mistress	Annie West
Playboy Boss, Pregnancy of Passion	Kate Hardy
A Night with the Society Playboy	Ally Blake
One Night with the Rebel Billionaire	Trish Wylie
Two Weeks in the Magnate's Bed	Nicola Marsh
Magnate's Mistress…Accidentally Pregnant	Kimberly Lang
Desert Prince, Blackmailed Bride	Kim Lawrence
The Nurse's Baby Miracle	Janice Lynn
Second Lover	Gill Sanderson

HISTORICAL

The Rake and the Heiress	Marguerite Kaye
Wicked Captain, Wayward Wife	Sarah Mallory
The Pirate's Willing Captive	Anne Herries

MEDICAL™

Angel's Christmas	Caroline Anderson
Someone To Trust	Jennifer Taylor
Morrison's Magic	Abigail Gordon
Wedding Bells	Meredith Webber

MILLS & BOON®

FEBRUARY 2010 LARGE PRINT TITLES

ROMANCE

Desert Prince, Bride of Innocence	Lynne Graham
Raffaele: Taming His Tempestuous Virgin	Sandra Marton
The Italian Billionaire's Secretary Mistress	Sharon Kendrick
Bride, Bought and Paid For	Helen Bianchin
Betrothed: To the People's Prince	Marion Lennox
The Bridesmaid's Baby	Barbara Hannay
The Greek's Long-Lost Son	Rebecca Winters
His Housekeeper Bride	Melissa James

HISTORICAL

The Brigadier's Daughter	Catherine March
The Wicked Baron	Sarah Mallory
His Runaway Maiden	June Francis

MEDICAL™

Emergency: Wife Lost and Found	Carol Marinelli
A Special Kind of Family	Marion Lennox
Hot-Shot Surgeon, Cinderella Bride	Alison Roberts
A Summer Wedding at Willowmere	Abigail Gordon
Miracle: Twin Babies	Fiona Lowe
The Playboy Doctor Claims His Bride	Janice Lynn

millsandboon.co.uk Community

Join Us!

The Community is the perfect place to meet and chat to kindred spirits who love books and reading as much as you do, but it's also the place to:

- **Get the inside scoop from authors about their latest books**
- **Learn how to write a romance book with advice from our editors**
- **Help us to continue publishing the best in women's fiction**
- **Share your thoughts on the books we publish**
- **Befriend other users**

Forums: Interact with each other as well as authors, editors and a whole host of other users worldwide.

Blogs: Every registered community member has their own blog to tell the world what they're up to and what's on their mind.

Book Challenge: We're aiming to read 5,000 books and have joined forces with The Reading Agency in our inaugural Book Challenge.

Profile Page: Showcase yourself and keep a record of your recent community activity.

Social Networking: We've added buttons at the end of every post to share via digg, Facebook, Google, Yahoo, Technorati and de.licio.us.

www.millsandboon.co.uk

COMMUNITY HB